THE REBELLION BEGINS

BASED ON "SPARK OF REBELLION"
TELEPLAY BY SIMON KINBERG
ADAPTED BY MICHAEL KOGGE

Disney

LUCASFILM
P R E S S

Los Angeles • New York

*To new hopes
and new beginnings*

Printed in the United States of America

First Edition
1 3 5 7 9 10 8 6 4 2
V475-2873-0-14248

Library of Congress Control Number: 2014937127
ISBN 978-1-4847-1475-1

Visit www.starwars.com

SUSTAINABLE
FORESTRY
INITIATIVE

Certified Chain of Custody
Promoting Sustainable Forestry

www.sfiprogram.org
SFI-01054
The SFI label applies to the text stock

"You say you are an orphan, without a friend in the world; all the inquiries I have been able to make, confirm the statement. Let me hear your story; where you come from; who brought you up; and how you got into the company in which I found you. Speak the truth, and you shall not be friendless while I live."

—Charles Dickens, *Oliver Twist*

CONTENTS

PROLOGUE

TWO ghosts haunted the depths of the Outer Rim.

Both were star vessels, converging in space. One was large, nearly corvette-class, and bore a unique design that might be most likened to a manual crossbow. Its wide, circular prow protruded from a rectangular midsection, along which projected an assortment of weaponry, from laser cannons to missile launchers. It would be classified as a gunship, though none of its guns moved as the other vessel crept up to its airlock. It seemed to be nothing more than a derelict drifting in space, its cockpit dark, its hull ruptured by blaster holes, its engines cold, a ghost of its former self.

The docking vessel—a bulky, hexagonal freighter of Corellian origin—was a ghost of another kind. Equipped with baffled engines, energy dampeners, and static jammers, the freighter had been modified to be deliberately hard to detect. Sensors frequently registered it

1

as a solar fluctuation or cosmic radiation rather than a starship.

Its crew called it the *Ghost*.

Kanan Jarrus stood in the *Ghost*'s docking tube, surrounded by his four crewmates. All eyes, photoreceptors, and blasters were fixed on the gunship's airlock. Everyone was on edge, even him.

They had traveled to this remote part of the Rim to converse with the gunship's captain, on the advice of Cikatro Vizago, a Devaronian crime lord on Lothal with whom both were acquainted. This captain allegedly shared the same anti-Imperial views as the *Ghost*'s ragtag bunch and was seeking to coordinate efforts in his fight against the Empire. Desiring to take their own struggle beyond the planet Lothal, Kanan and his colleague Hera Syndulla had agreed to meet the captain, so Vizago had arranged it to happen here in deep space.

Unfortunately, given the exterior damage the gunship had taken, it appeared that the Empire—or someone with the appropriate firepower—had arrived there first. This made Kanan and his crewmates wary, since either enemy or ally could be on the other side of the airlock.

"Five, four," Sabine said, counting down the timer

of the detonation charges she'd placed on the airlock. In her Mandalorian armor and helmet, the girl was the most protected of all of them—yet also would be the first one noticed in a potential firefight. Swirls of purple, pink, and orange dappled her helmet and plates, a pattern that would work as camouflage only in a graffiti-covered undercity.

"One," she said. The charges blew, right on time.

Kanan held his breath and squinted through the smoke. No one appeared in the airlock. The gunship corridor beyond was dark. "Chopper, scan for any life signs."

The crew's mechanical member, the barrel-shaped astromech droid C1-10P, grumbled as he rolled forward and rotated his battered orange-and-yellow dome. While most astromech units whistled or tweedled to communicate in place of expensive vocabulators, Chopper favored lower tones. He grunted back an all clear.

"*Karabast*," cursed Zeb in his native tongue. The brawny Lasat stooped in the docking tube, the tips of his sharp ears touching the ceiling. He pulled at his chin curtain of beard. "I was hopin' for some Imps. I could do with a little head bashing right now."

"Be careful what you wish for, Garazeb Orrelios,"

Hera said. "One day it might be your head that's bashed. Maybe then someone can knock a little sense into you."

Kanan smirked. Hera always knew how to lighten grave situations. She claimed her sarcasm was a Twi'lek trait, like her ability to communicate solely through the movements of her *lekku* head-tails. But Kanan had encountered many serious members of her species who had no sense of humor. Her dry wit came from living a life constantly in peril. If you couldn't look death in the face and laugh a little, she often said, then you were probably already dead.

"What do you think?" he asked her.

"I'm as clueless as you," Hera said. "Everyone could be vaped aboard that ship—or it could be a trap. Perhaps you could—"

Kanan shot her down abruptly. "No."

Her green head-tails twitched in annoyance. She could be as irritated as she wanted to be, but he wasn't going to be pressured into doing what she was implying. She didn't comprehend what that might cost, not just to him, but all of them.

"Well, I'm not going to stand here when I could be redecorating the gunship," Sabine said, her helmet filtering none of the sass from her voice.

Kanan held her back from going into the airlock

first. "Save your art and just hang on to your blasters," he said. "Hera, Chopper, keep the *Ghost* warm in case we need a quick getaway. And inform Vizago about what happened to his 'acquaintances.'"

"Already sent the message," Hera said, and turned with the droid. She was disappointed in him, he could tell. But she'd get over it, like she always did.

Gesturing Zeb and Sabine to follow, Kanan strode through the dissipating smoke into the airlock. Since the gunship's emergency lights were out, he activated his glowrod.

What he saw astounded him. The corridor seemed to be constructed not of steel, but wood. And not just any ordinary wood. The wood used here remained in its natural state, without varnish or sanding, as if freshly cut from a tree. Branches and limbs curled out at various angles, forming arches or conduits for hidden wiring. Huge circular knots adorned the walls like gallery portraits. Thick slices of trunk made for bulkheads, while sap served as caulking and glue for the integrated technology. Kanan had never seen such handcrafted beauty.

"I shouldn't have suggested tagging these walls," Sabine said. "This is true art."

"But where are the artists?" Zeb asked, warily sniffing the air.

They turned down the corridor and entered an enormous chamber that housed a lattice of stocky tree limbs. Some branches were bare like wood beams, while others were covered with a clumpy moss. They stretched across the chamber in multiple levels, woven together to form a network so thick Kanan could not see the ceiling.

"Thought I smelled *wroshyr* wood," Zeb said.

"You've been to the forests of Kashyyyk?" Sabine asked.

"No. But the Wookiees who came to fight the Imperial invasion on Lasan all had weapons whittled from the *wroshyr* trees of their home."

Kanan stroked his goatee. "Interesting. So Vizago's freedom fighters are Wookiees, and this is—was—their gunship." He recalled some Wookiees he had known, and how they preferred resting in trees rather than bunks. The branches here must serve as the beds of their sleeping cabin.

"Makes sense the Wookiees would arm themselves and fight back. The Empire took over Kashyyyk, like it did Mandalore," Sabine said.

"And Lasan," Zeb snarled.

Kanan put his hand on a limb. The moss crumbled off, dead. No one had slept here in a while, for Wookiees fastidiously maintained their living environments. On the bare limb below, however, he noticed a series of pictographic marks that had been scratched into the bark. "Is this writing?"

Zeb and Sabine went over to look. "Definitely Wookiee," Zeb said. "I saw similar markings on their weapons. Wish I could read it."

"It says 'Kitwarr, son of . . . Wullffwarro,' or at least I think so," Sabine said.

"You can read Wookiee?" Kanan and Zeb asked at once, both surprised.

"A little. Part of the elementary Mandalorian curriculum, along with Huttese, Aqualish, and a dozen other languages," Sabine said with a shrug. "Can't speak any Wookiee, though. No human can. We don't have their throats."

Zeb traced the markings with a finger. "Wullffwarro. I know that name. He was one of the Republic's greatest soldiers during the Clone Wars."

"I remember his name, too. He was always on the holonews, but when the Empire was declared, he suddenly disappeared," Kanan said, interrupted by what sounded like a cough.

They all quieted and looked about. It *was* a cough, coming from farther inside the ship. Someone was still alive, probably at the brink of death.

Kanan led the others under the branches toward the

source of the sound. They went through an arched portal and came out onto the gunship's bridge.

Unlike the other pristine sections of the ship, the bridge was a disaster area. The benches before the various stations had been yanked from their moorings. All the technical systems were in pieces, shattered and smashed. Red and green blood smeared the cracked viewport and stained the *wroshyr* wood trim. A ferocious battle had been fought here, yet oddly, only one body lay among the rubble.

It was not a Wookiee. It was the sworn enemy of all Wookiees.

It was a Trandoshan.

"Slaver," Zeb roared.

Kanan held Zeb back from strangling the reptilian humanoid. The Trandoshan's wounds would bring an end to his suffering soon enough. His green flight suit was pitted with palm-sized holes, probably from a Wookiee bowcaster, and he was shedding orange scales faster than he could regenerate them.

Kanan knelt beside him. "Where are the Wookiees?"

One of the Trandoshan's eyes stayed closed, but the other rolled toward Kanan. His serpentine tongue flicked in and out of his mouth as he rasped his final breaths.

Kanan caught the Trandoshan's tongue. "Where?"

The Trandoshan gurgled, unable to speak until Kanan released his tongue. The reptilian spat out a last word. "Empire."

Zeb howled and reached down to pick up the slaver with one hand. "You sold them to the Imps, you savage?"

The Trandoshan couldn't answer, no matter how hard Zeb shook him. He was already dead.

Kanan touched Zeb's shoulder. "Calm yourself."

Zeb steamed, but dropped the slaver's corpse back on the ground. "We need to find them. We need to save the Wookiees."

The rangefinder antenna on Sabine's helmet rotated. "Hera's heard back from Vizago," she said, then paused for a few moments. "He's looking into what happened here. In the meantime, he's got a job for us. An Imperial supply grab that should be simple and will pay handsomely."

Kanan frowned. Nothing was simple when it came to Cikatro Vizago and his jobs. "Do I even need to guess where this pickup is?"

Even with the helmet on, everyone could hear the smile in Sabine's voice. "Where else would it be?"

"Lothal," Zeb growled.

PART I
LOTHAL

CHAPTER 1

There was a saying among traders in the Outer Rim that you hadn't seen the color green until you'd landed in the grasslands of Lothal. Though Ezra Bridger hadn't been to any other planet—he was only fourteen, after all—he doubted he'd ever dispute that saying. The grass on Lothal had the sheen of gold.

And it was everywhere, as far as the eye could see. Barring the occasional mound and mountain range, vast prairies spanned Lothal's continents like great seas of golden green.

Ezra gunned his jump bike through one of these seas, racing across the grasslands beyond Capital City. The speed of the ride thrilled him. His hair flapped in front of his eyes, his heart raced, and the mounds whipped past him like he imagined the starlines of hyperspace would.

He took the freeway for a stretch, then got off at the

exit for the spaceport. Transports, passenger shuttles, and freighters of all kinds landed on and launched from the berthing bays. One day he, too, would be piloting a ship of his own, hopping from planet to planet, never staying anywhere too long, doing all his trading by himself, a lone operator in the great galaxy.

After parking the bike in a distant lot, he took a speeder bus to the spaceport proper. The place was bustling and getting busier by the day. Humans and nonhumans of a dozen species that Ezra couldn't name hurried between terminals that offered flights to such glamorous worlds as Corellia, Ryloth, and Imperial Center, where one huge metropolis covered the entire planet. Holographic billboards promoted even more exotic destinations and advertised everything from the latest gardening droids to the local Imperial Academy. The ever-increasing activity was due in no small part to the also ever-increasing military presence of the Empire on Lothal. Flat-winged TIE fighters patrolled the skies while white-armored stormtroopers patrolled the spaceport and city. The added security dulled Lothal's reputation as a frontier world and lured wealthy Imperial citizens to come and relocate their businesses, start new ventures, or even take a holiday.

It also made Ezra especially vigilant. Being caught

for crimes as minor as petty theft could get him locked up in an Imperial prison where he could labor for years unpaid as a slave.

This meant Ezra had to keep a low profile in the more secure areas, like the spaceport. With his backpack strapped around his shoulders, he pretended to be just another traveler as he roamed the crowds, fishing for the perfect mark to pickpocket. Desperate as he was for credits, he prided himself on stealing only from those who appeared more fortunate than he was. On Lothal, the fortunate were usually Imperials. Making off with a comlink or an officer's rank pin could earn him enough at a pawn shop to pay for a week's meals.

"Ezra Bridger?" piped a voice behind him. "By the Z'gag, it is you!"

Three tiny hands caught a strap dangling from his backpack and pulled Ezra out of the crowd. A larva-like Ruurian with sixteen limbs, stunted wings, and large multifaceted eyes wormed up before him.

Ezra frowned. "Hello, Slyyth."

The Ruurian clacked his mandibles, his species' version of a smile. "What a coincidence! I was just thinking how useful your talents would be for a job I have in mind."

"You know I don't work for anyone."

"Ezra, Ezra," Slyyth said, brushing his feathery

antennae against Ezra's cheek. "Just let me tell you the details. It's only a snatch-and-run."

Ezra stepped back from the antennae in disgust. "Last time you said that, I nearly got caught in an Imperial sting operation. No thanks."

"But the credits we could make—"

Slyyth erupted into spasms of violent coughs. Woolly hair began to fall off his tubular body, which was blemished by yellow splotches Ezra hadn't seen before.

"Are you ill?"

"Worse," Slyyth said. "If I can't afford another treatment, I might not be slithering on the ground for much longer."

Ezra didn't know much about Ruurians, except that at a certain advanced age they spun a cocoon around themselves, shed their larval forms, and became beautiful chroma-wings. They considered this transformation to be Paradise—a phase during which one's sole desires were eating, mating, and flying along the banks of Ruuria's pink rivers. Slyyth, however, found the idea terrifying. He wouldn't be able to fence stolen goods and make a profit if all he wanted to do was flutter over a riverbank. So for years, he had denied himself from entering the final stage of his biology by using various ointments, taking prescriptions, and getting special treatments.

"Whatever you're taking is making you sick," Ezra said.

"Sick is better than gone," Slyyth said.

"You won't be gone. You'll be free to do what all your species do, and you won't have to worry about making ends meet any longer," Ezra said. The more he thought about it, the more becoming a chroma-wing really didn't sound like that bad of a proposition.

"But the credits, the credits. I'll never be rich—" The Ruurian broke into another series of coughs.

"Good-bye, Slyyth." Ezra started to walk away.

"It's a shame," Slyyth said, managing to get his coughs under control. "You're an artful little dodger, more talented than any pickpocket I know—including old Slyyth in his prime—but you're as stubborn as a pupa." He sighed and his antennae drooped. "Guess I'll just have to ask Kinsdaw or Tesba if they can snatch the helmets."

Ezra stopped. "Helmets?"

Slyyth let out a couple of weak coughs. He produced a flimsi in one hand. "According to the manifest I acquired, it's part of a shipment for the new bucket-heads at the Academy."

"*Stormtrooper* helmets?" Now Ezra was intrigued. "Where?"

Slyyth drew to his full height and clacked his mandibles. He wasn't coughing anymore.

Ezra crept through the spaceport's access corridors, staying away from random Imperial patrols. He came to the emergency door to bay 49 and used the astromech arm he kept in his backpack to pick the lock. He slipped inside the bay to find Academy cadets unloading cargo from an Imperial transport like labor droids. They carried off crates of foodstuffs, canisters of cleaning solutions, and bags of refurbished stormtrooper armor while the Supply Master, a turgid fellow named Lyste with whom Ezra had had a few run-ins, screamed at them to move faster.

Slyyth had assured him the Imperials wouldn't be there for another half hour, so he could just walk into the transport, snatch the bags, and hurry out. That obviously wasn't going to be the case. Yet despite the chance of being caught, Ezra didn't leave. His instincts told him to stay. He trusted these inner feelings more than anything or anyone else, since they always nudged him to pick the deepest pockets and guided him through rough and risky circumstances. They compelled Ezra to wait, so he did, ducking behind chemical barrels to see if an opportunity would arise.

The opportunity did when Lyste pulled an unfortunate cadet out of line and berated her. Ezra sprinted out, took her place, and marched into the transport.

"Overslept, forgot my uniform," he whispered to the cadets around him. "Hopefully there'll be one on the transport. Last thing I want is disciplinary action from Lyste."

"Got that right," said a cadet. "If I get one more bad mark on my record, he's threatened to transfer me to the spice mines of Kessel."

Kessel. It was one place Ezra never wanted to visit. Other than death, being sent to its spice mines was as bad a punishment as the Empire could deliver.

Once they were aboard the transport, a cadet tossed Ezra an extra uniform from a crate. Ezra flipped him a credit in thanks and then grabbed the two bags that corresponded with the ones that contained helmets on Slyyth's manifest. Excusing himself to change into the uniform, he veered into the ship's corridor, found a portside hatch, and exited.

He came out near the refueling hose and crouched behind it to slink back to the emergency door. When Lyste's eyes were elsewhere, he opened the door and dashed out, hastening down the access corridor, away from the docking bay.

He dropped off the bag that was Slyyth's cut in a rusty refuse bin and trekked across the spaceport lots to his jump bike. The bag fit in the storage compartment behind the seat, and Ezra was off, zooming down the freeway and into the grasslands toward his hideout.

Soon the old communications tower came into view, rising over the prairie like a lighthouse. Ezra slowed the bike. Once this tower had been linked to a vast grid that coordinated air travel between the planet's scattered settlements, until it was supplanted by a more advanced Imperial network. Now what stood was little more than a rusted relic, stripped of valuable equipment long before by scrap thieves and overgrown by green daisies.

All this made the tower the perfect hideout.

Ezra didn't need access to high-tech communications systems. Contact with the outside world was the last thing he wanted. Located outside the capital city, the tower served as his personal sanctuary from the urban chaos. Here Ezra could be by himself—and *be* himself. The tower was the one place he could call home.

He parked the bike inside the garage and got off the seat, his legs a little numb from the ride. Bits of technology, most of it of Imperial manufacture, littered the floor like in a mechanic's shop. Ammo-less blasters and stormtrooper rifles dangled on a rack. A shuttle stabilizer had been shoved between cargo containers, while the base of a Treadwell droid, missing its tread, occupied the corner with two broken jump boots. Other components, from power couplings to circuit boards, in various states of disrepair cluttered a workbench.

None of that stuff really mattered to Ezra. His most treasured possessions were his Imperial helmets, neatly arranged on shelves and lockers as if for a museum display. His most recent acquisition, a TIE fighter pilot's helmet, hung front and center atop a jacket rack.

Now he had more to add. He pulled out the bag from the bike's storage compartment, untied it, and turned it over. Instead of helmets, holopads spilled out.

He almost kicked himself. He hadn't had time to check the bags. He'd just assumed what the manifest declared was correct. He sifted through the holopads, finding nothing else, not even blaster packs or biker goggles. He didn't understand it. What would a military supply transport be doing with holopads?

He picked up one of the holopads and thumbed the tiny button. A three-dimensional image of two happy parents and their son was projected from its surface. "You, too, can be part of the Imperial family," announced a pompous voice from the holopad's micro-speaker. "Don't just dream about applying for the Academy; make it come true. You can find a career in space—Exploration, Starfleet, or Merchant Service. Choose from Navigation, Engineering, Space Medicine, Contact/Liaison, and more."

Having heard the same commercial at the spaceport over the years, Ezra knew the words by heart. "If you have the right stuff to take on the universe and standardized examination scores that meet requirements," he recited along, mimicking the adult voice and its upper-crust accent, "dispatch your application to the Academy screening office, care of the Commandant, and join the ranks of the proud!"

Ezra clicked his tongue along with the concluding drumroll, then stopped, realizing that he was parroting Imperial propaganda. He lifted his thumb in sudden revulsion. The picture disappeared and the micro-speaker silenced, though the words stayed in his head. The ad was like a bad tune you couldn't forget, which was the point. The Empire wanted everyone in his generation to think the same, dream the same, be the same, like little Imperial droids.

He tossed the holopad onto his workbench. Ezra wouldn't be one of their droids. He wasn't anyone's droid.

His stomach growled, reminding him he hadn't eaten. He reached into a soldier's helmet that he'd re-purposed as a fruit bowl and found he had only one jogan left when he thought he had two. The fruit was squishy and overripe, but he was hungry enough to eat grass at this point.

Ezra jammed the jogan under his arm and climbed the ladder to the observation deck, where he could eat in peace and watch the stars come out.

CHAPTER 2

Many kilometers above Lothal's night sky, a shuttle departed hyperspace. Yet the thousands of lights that greeted the shuttle weren't the twinkling dots of the cosmos. They shone from the massive triangular form of the Imperial Star Destroyer *Lawbringer,* which floated against the planet's blue-green sphere like a vibrospear poised to stake fresh ground.

The shuttle's pilot grinned. He had come out from hyperspace at the precise location he'd calculated— right over the Star Destroyer's bridge, where its captain would be standing, frozen in shock.

"Unknown shuttle, identify yourself immediately, or be blasted," barked a voice over his subspace comm.

The pilot spoke calmly into the comm, not rattled by the threat. "Agent Kallus of the ISB, requesting permission to dock."

There was hesitation on the other end; then the

comm officer spoke in a more respectful tone. "Please hold, sir."

Kallus swooped the shuttle to fly over the bridge a second time. The Star Destroyer's turbolasers tracked him, but wisely the gunners never fired. The mere mention of the Imperial Security Bureau made men think twice about what they were doing.

Another voice came over the comm, with an aristocrat's accent. "This is Captain Zataire of the *Lawbringer*. I offer my sincerest apologies, Agent Kallus. We weren't expecting you. It doesn't appear that you were on the flight schedule."

"I wasn't," Kallus said. He was never on the schedule. His visit, like all his visits, was meant to be a surprise. "Where shall I dock?"

Zataire's voice quavered. "The aft hangar. I will be there to meet you. Cut your sublight engines so the tractor beam can get a lock."

"No need to use the tractor beam. I will land the shuttle myself."

"As you wish. It will be a pleasure to have you aboard."

Kallus knew that pleasure was the last thing the captain was feeling right then. Dread would be the more appropriate emotion. For the ISB to board your ship was not exactly an honor any commander wanted.

Though he held no military rank, as a full executive agent, Kallus had the authority to countermand any of the captain's orders if it helped fulfill his mission to hunt down and catch potential rebels.

The Star Destroyer's bay doors opened. Kallus glided his shuttle toward them, maintaining a slower-than-average speed. Every second of his approach would amplify Zataire's dread. Every second would remind the captain that he had just lost his ship.

The *Lawbringer* was, for all practical purposes, now Kallus's to command.

Captain Hiram Zataire loved his emerald wine. He poured glass after glass during the dinner he hosted for Kallus in his ornately decorated cabin. Zataire spent most of the meal detailing the qualities of his favorite vintages, commenting that for as green as Lothal was, its emerald grapes often tasted as sour as Hutt punch. Kallus sipped his wine and nodded politely, offering an occasional question to keep the captain babbling. Small talk frequently revealed more about a man than direct interrogation did. Before Kallus made his next move, he had to learn if Zataire was whom his Imperial datafile said he was, a somewhat fussy yet fiercely loyal officer of the Empire. He needed to know if the captain could be trusted.

Zataire twice brought up his vineyard on Naboo, of which there was no record in his datafile. The file did report that Zataire owned a couple of large plantations on the planet, so Kallus assumed the vineyard was part of those properties. The file also noted that Zataire had a wife and three children, two daughters and a son. The captain spoke glowingly of his wife, who stayed married to him even while he was away on these long assignments, and his daughters, who were the dearest things in his life. The eldest shared his passion for wine and ran the vineyard, while her sister had followed his footsteps into the armed forces and was serving as a lieutenant aboard Lord Tion's flagship, the *Devastator*.

Of his son, he made no mention.

As they ate, Kallus surveyed the cabin in quick glances and long, pensive looks. He had trained himself to assess people's loyalty by profiling everything around them. He took note of their possessions, the arrangement of their habitation spaces, the quality of their cutlery, how and where they hung their hats—anything unique that made them stand out, or, even better, the things that didn't. Because in Kallus's experience, the things that didn't stand out in plain view were often the very things people wanted to hide.

The captain's refined tastes went beyond emerald wine. Ivory bantha bone framed a floor-to-ceiling viewport that offered a gorgeous vista of Lothal. A chromatic chandelier hovering above the dining table cycled through variations of colors that complemented the planet's blue-green glow. Shelved along the wall, and sorted by topic and author, were books—not data-tapes or flimsiplast replicas, but collector's hard copies, ink printed on paper. Kallus had never seen so many of them outside a library. Dust even lingered on a spine or two.

These furnishings made for impressive quarters. Zataire was evidently a man of independent means, as a captain's pay grade could never afford such extrava-gances. Kallus judged he most likely served the Navy for the privilege of his rank rather than any finan-cial gain. Such men were rarely disloyal, since they feared risking the respect they had gained among their peers. In fact, they made some of the Empire's best commanders—wealthy citizens who were not blue-bloods by birth but had joined the upper classes by climbing the military ladder.

The only thing that stood out to Kallus was the wine.

When Zataire went to refill their glasses, Kallus made his move. "I must ask, Captain, if you despise Lothal's emerald wine so much, why do you keep pour-ing it?"

Zataire's hands shook almost imperceptibly as he held the bottle. Kallus continued before the man could answer. "Might it be because the wine is not a vintage from Lothal at all, but one from Alderaan?" He sneered when he said the name of the world. Alderaan had been a constant thorn in the Empire's side. The planet's government, led by the House of Organa, had repeatedly argued against the military crackdowns required to maintain order. They claimed to champion peace but in reality only fomented anarchy.

Zataire's voice trembled with his hands. "I . . . did not realize you, too, were a wine connoisseur."

"My job necessitates I be an expert at many things. Let me have that before you drop it." Kallus took the bottle of wine from Zataire. The label showed it came from a vineyard on Lothal, but Kallus peeled that off to reveal another label beneath.

"Just as I thought. From the Organa Ranch on Alderaan," Kallus said.

"I dare not serve a man of your standing the local Hutt punch," Zataire said. "That was the only bottle I had that wasn't from Lothal, a gift I recently received."

"From that rebel you call a son, perhaps?" Kallus casually asked.

The stem of the wineglass snapped in Zataire's hand. Bright green liquid spilled all over the tablecloth.

"Are you accusing me of disloyalty, Agent Kallus?"

"Captain, I haven't accused you of anything. That is something I do only when the facts give me reason to. As an agent of the ISB, I follow the letter of the law."

Zataire held the broken wineglass in his hand, his mouth half open. Kallus poured the last of the bottle into his own glass, which he then offered to Zataire. "You should enjoy this while you can. As bothersome as Alderaan may be, I agree, her vintages are the best. But one wonders how much longer her grapes will grow."

Zataire took a moment to accept Kallus's glass. "Please know I despise my son's political views," he said. "But I love him and could not refuse his gift. It is what any good father would do."

"Of course it is. And as a good Imperial, you have provided me the location of your rebellious child. You know we have been looking for him for years."

Zataire sighed. "My son has a big mouth and is prone to outrageous speeches, but he's not a rebel. He'll see the value of the New Order when he grows older. Please do not hurt him."

"Captain Zataire, the Imperial Security Bureau was created to protect the Empire's citizens, especially the children of a decorated officer like yourself. The last thing we'd ever want is for him to be kidnapped for ransom, or, worse yet, tortured and killed. As you are probably well aware, Alderaan can be a rough place, with all the anti-Imperials lurking about."

Zataire swirled the wine in his glass, then put it down without drinking. He did not look at Kallus when he spoke. "Might there be a way to guarantee my son's safety?"

Kallus paused, as if considering Zataire's request. In truth, he had already gamed out this conversation—and what he could offer in return for Zataire's full support. He didn't need to offer anything, since his jurisdiction gave him the authority to order the captain to do whatever was required to accomplish the mission. But going over the captain's head would make Zataire an enemy, one who would stall in securing him any necessary resources. And Kallus didn't come to Lothal to battle fellow Imperials. He came to root out rebels.

"The galaxy is a dangerous place, as you well know, and safety can never be fully guaranteed. But the letter of the law allows, shall I say, a certain flexibility in both of our duties." Kallus leaned toward Zataire. "If you give me your fullest cooperation, without any bureaucratic nonsense, I will do my utmost to personally ensure that your son's big mouth does not get him into further trouble."

Zataire stared into his wine before finally lifting his head and looking Kallus in the eye. "You've always had my fullest cooperation, Agent Kallus."

"Which I never questioned. You are a fine Imperial, Captain Zataire. If we end the subversive activity on Lothal, you will be commended. But first things first. Have the *Lawbringer* descend through the atmosphere to hover over the capital city. The locals should tremble when they see the magnificent weapons we wield."

"You want us to leave orbit? The planet will go unprotected." It was the only time during the dinner Zataire had raised his voice, a sign that he took his duty seriously.

"Unprotected from whom? There is no imminent threat of invasion anywhere in the galaxy. Like never before, space itself is at peace, because of the Empire's might."

Kallus turned in his chair toward the viewport. Since he had boarded the Star Destroyer, Lothal had made a half rotation, bringing dawn to its other side. Now its major continents blazed a brilliant green.

Kallus narrowed his eyes like lasers at the planet. "The one and only danger to our beloved Empire, my dear captain," he said, "lies not from without, but from within."

To eliminate rebel activity once and for all on Lothal, he would bleed those lands red.

CHAPTER 3

Ezra woke to the rumble of thunder. He staggered to his feet, woozy after having spent the whole night asleep on the observation deck. It wasn't raining yet, so he blinked away the last bits of sleep from his eyes and went over to the tower's edge. Leaning his arms against the railing, he looked out at the dawn.

Green daisies had sprouted around the tower, waiting to bloom. Insects buzzed about the flat prairie, some snatched from the air by swift paws of furry rodents. In the distance loomed Capital City, where smokestacks pumped pollutants into the sky. The morning cloud layer glowed its usual purple haze. Oddly, Ezra didn't see any sign of rain, though the rumbling continued. Some of it came from his stomach, which craved more than the previous night's jogan. But most of the rumble came from above. Ezra tilted his gaze—and dropped his jaw.

An Imperial Star Destroyer soared overhead.

The ship was colossal, far bigger than it appeared on news reports. Over a kilometer and a half long, it darkened the sky and seemed endless. Giant turbolaser batteries projected from its armor-plated belly, all pointed in one direction—toward Capital City.

Ezra pictured the city's well-to-do citizens cheering the oncoming craft while the poorer denizens scurried into whatever hole they could find. They were the wise ones. An Imperial Star Destroyer approaching one's home was not generally a positive sign.

A squadron of TIE fighters launched from the Star Destroyer's hangar. Some shot off toward the city, while others circled the vessel like bloodflies around a nerf. Ezra squatted to the deck floor as one fighter swooped close by. He doubted the pilot had seen him. TIEs were always zipping back and forth over the prairies, patrolling for rebel activity. Their constant presence required Ezra to dim the tower's illumination so as not to attract attention.

The Star Destroyer's bulk terminated in a set of conical ion engines. The brightness forced Ezra to shield his eyes. Nonetheless, it did not stop him from seeing the prospects that now lay before him. Whatever drew a warship of this size might not be positive, but it could be immensely profitable. There would be many Imperials running about, which would present lots of pockets—and helmets—to pick.

After his last botched effort, he wanted those helmets more than ever.

Ezra scrambled down the ladder, grabbed his backpack, and started his jump bike, his hunger forgotten.

Ezra hid his bike in a deserted alley and waded into the crowded city bazaar. There citizens of all stripes bustled and mingled, bartering for spare parts or scavenging discount bins for the best deals. Down row after row of stalls, merchants hawked a galaxy's trove of goods, offering cut-rate prices on secondhand trinkets. For the famished, street cooks roasted sweetmeats on sticks and farmers sold their harvests of fruits and vegetables. More than one fat wallet stood out as an easy grab, but Ezra held back. He was searching for Imperials.

It didn't take him long to find them. Ahead, a surge of marketgoers tried to leave. Imperials always caused that reaction in people.

He elbowed past two swine-snouted Ugnaughts, then crouched behind tall clay casks. Strutting past him in olive uniforms were a pair of Imperial officers whom everyone knew by name: Commandant Aresko and his lackey, Taskmasker Grint. Assigned to run Lothal's

Imperial Academy, the two spent their free time doing whatever they could to make life miserable for the inhabitants of the lower levels. Today their victim was Yoffar, an old Gotal who eked out a living peddling yesterday's fruits.

"Your identification. Now," Grint ordered, pushing his barrel of a belly near the Gotal's horns.

Yoffar held up a plump specimen from his basket. "I'm just trying to sell a couple jogans here."

"Did you say *sell*?" asked Aresko, who held his nose high like a prince. "You do realize that all trade must be registered with the Empire."

The Gotal snorted. "By the time the Empire's done, there won't be any trade left."

Grint stepped closer to Yoffar, sneering. "What did you say?"

Ezra felt sorry for Yoffar. Truthfully, he'd never liked the geezer. The white-furred fruit seller was a perpetual grump who always confused Ezra with the other street orphans and once had accused Ezra of nicking fruit, which Ezra hadn't—not *that* day, at least. But no one, not even Yoffar for all his crankiness, deserved Imperial harassment for trying to get by. Perhaps there was something Ezra could do—or steal—to turn the tables.

If the Gotal felt harassed and intimidated, he didn't

show it. "I remember what it was like before your ships showed up, before you Imperials ruled Lothal like the rest of the galaxy."

Grint glanced at Aresko. Neither could hide his glee. "Mister Grint," Aresko said with a raised eyebrow. "That sounds like treasonous talk to me."

"That it does, sir," said Grint.

Aresko unclipped his comlink from his belt. It was one of the new Imperial editions, built to transmit across a range of frequencies, including coded military bands. Although it wasn't a helmet, Ezra could make a nice chunk of credits pawning it and have some fun at the same time.

"This is L-R-C-zero-one," Aresko said into his comlink. "I'm bringing in a citizen under suspicion of treason."

A voice responded almost instantaneously, the same electronically modulated voice that could be heard across the galaxy—an Imperial stormtrooper. "Copy that, L-R-C-zero-one. Dispatch to cell block A-A-thirty-three."

The clatter of boots prompted Ezra to glance behind him. Two white-armored stormtroopers marched through the market, already en route. This wasn't some chance license check—this was a stunt, planned to demonstrate the Empire's speed at responding to incidents in order to strike fear into the hearts of onlookers. Fear was how Imperials tried to handle everything.

Ezra wasn't afraid.

He slinked along the line of clay casks, judging the best way to approach Aresko. The commandant had reattached the comlink to his belt. Ezra could pinch it if he came from the side. He slipped behind the stormtroopers and used them as cover.

Grint took a fruit from Yoffar's basket. "By Imperial authority, we hereby confiscate your goods."

Old Yoffar's bravado became slack-jawed terror when he saw the stormtroopers approaching him. "Take him away," ordered Aresko.

The troopers grabbed the Gotal and began to drag him off. Yoffar clutched the fruit basket to his chest. "You can't do this!"

Grint took a bite of the jogan he'd stolen as he and Aresko followed the stormtroopers. "Yeah? And who's gonna stop us?" He pointed at other merchants around them. "You? *You?*"

The merchants looked away, some packing up their merchandise. Ezra sidled up to Grint. "Hey, mister, spare a jogan?"

Both Imperials turned and Ezra reached toward

Aresko's belt. His fingers made the lightest touch on the clip release, and the comlink was in his possession in less than a second.

"Scram, urchin. Those jogans are Imperial property," Grint said.

"Sorry, sorry. Not looking for trouble, sirs." Ezra lowered his head so they couldn't see his face and hurried away. "But it sure has a way of finding me," he said under his breath. Because he wasn't done with them. He still had to have his fun.

He set the comlink to loudspeaker broadcast and cleared his throat. "All officers to the main square." He spoke into the comlink, impersonating the pompous adult voice from the holopad advertisements. "This is a code red emergency!"

Ezra kept walking, head low, and glanced back. The Imperials had stopped, clearly annoyed by the orders. Grint spit out jogan seeds. Aresko gave Yoffar an arrogant glare. "It's your lucky day, Lothal scum." He motioned to the stormtroopers. "You two, come with us. Leave that nonhuman stinker in the dirt where he belongs."

The stormtroopers dropped Yoffar and rushed off with the officers toward the square. Once they were gone, the entire market let out a sigh of relief. Business returned to usual.

Yoffar picked up himself and his fruit basket. Ezra approached, his stomach reminding him of his hunger. He spoke into the comlink again so the Imperials wouldn't return soon. "Stay on alert! Repeat, this is code red."

Yoffar saw him with the comlink, and instead of giving his usual grumpy frown, he smiled. He offered Ezra a jogan. "Thank you."

"No, thank *you*." Ezra opened his backpack and packed it with jogans from the basket.

Yoffar's smile vanished. "Wait, wait. What are you doing?"

Ezra heaved his backpack over his shoulder and winked at the old grump. "Hey, a kid's gotta eat."

He stepped onto a nearby crate, climbed up a support beam, then leapt onto the rooftop of a building. "Who is that kid?" he heard the Gotal say.

Ezra grinned. Maybe now Yoffar wouldn't confuse him with the other orphans.

CHAPTER 4

With his heavy pack bouncing on his back, Ezra hopped over several chimneys to cross the roof. From the other edge, he could peek down into the city's main square. He was curious to see how the Imperials would react to his little ploy on the comlink.

Down below, Supply Master Lyste addressed a group of stormtroopers as they grav-chained hover crates to several speeder bikes. "Make sure the repulsors stick to the bikes," Lyste said, doing none of the lifting himself. "I don't want to lose any of those crates."

The two stormtroopers from the market arrived with Aresko and Grint in tow, both out of breath. "What's the emergency?" Aresko wheezed.

"Emergency?" Lyste asked.

On the roof, Ezra grinned, seeing the outcome of his comlink prank. From every adjoining street and alley came stormtroopers, stampeding into the square like herds of prairie squirrels in the mating season. Lyste, Grint, and Aresko looked about, utterly perplexed.

Grint leveled a glare at Lyste. "You called a code red."

"I-I'm not sure what you mean," Lyste stammered. "My orders are to get these crates to the Imperial Portal."

"Well, get them loaded, then!" Commandant Aresko said, reddening with anger.

To Ezra's delight, Lyste lent his own hands in lifting a heavy crate. Grint and Aresko muttered to each other while the other stormtroopers bumbled about, testing their helmet comlinks, looking nothing like the crack troops they were supposed to be. Ezra almost felt bad for the whole bunch. Almost.

His gaze fell on the hover crates Lyste's contingent attached to the speeder bikes. Three troopers remained to the side, guarding the two largest crates of the cluster. It was hard to tell from Ezra's vantage point what the crates could possibly hold, but a guard that strong probably meant whatever was inside was valuable. He stepped toward the roof's edge for a closer view and crouched, careful not to be seen.

In the center of the square stood a ponytailed man

in a collared olive tunic that was tucked into sleek gray pants. Dark green armor plated his right shoulder and matched the gauntlet around his forearm below. His back was toward Ezra, but he turned to look up at the rooftops, as if he had felt Ezra's gaze. The man's chin sported a sharp goatee, yet his blue eyes were even sharper, cutting through everything he looked at.

Weirded out, Ezra stepped back from the edge, where he could still see the man, but where the man hopefully couldn't see him.

The man looked away from the roof to a muscular nonhuman who stood nearly a meter taller than everyone else in the square. Ezra couldn't identify the being's species, but whatever he was, Ezra didn't want to get on his bad side.

The ponytailed man tapped his thigh twice, to which the nonhuman responded by turning into an alley. The man then approached a girl wearing outrageously colored Mandalorian armor and again tapped his thigh. The Mandalorian repeated the tap on her leg while heading in the opposite direction. All three were now on the move.

Interesting. Was what they had tapped a secret code? Ezra looked back at Supply Master Lyste and the stormtroopers. They had finished loading all the hover crates and didn't notice the Mandalorian walking close to the furthermost speeder bike. She slid her hand under the bike and pressed a blinking round object to the chassis.

Ezra knew immediately what that object was. He covered his ears. The object stopped blinking and the speeder bike exploded.

The shock wave knocked Lyste and his troopers backward. The once-puzzled stormtroopers in the square rushed to the scene, now having a purpose. Lyste crawled up and pointed at the other parked speeder bikes.

"Get those crates out of here," he yelled. "Keep them secure, at all costs!"

At all costs. Ezra liked the sound of that. It meant he was right about the crates being valuable. He rose from his crouch and dashed across the rooftops, searching for the quickest way down.

He wasn't going to make it. A stormtrooper jumped onto the speeder bike with the two largest crates and took off toward a side street. Even with his knowledge of the rooftops, there was no way Ezra could outrun a speeder bike.

The speeder bike didn't make it out of the square, though. Its rider screeched it to a halt to avoid colliding with a landspeeder that was backing out from a side street. The rider gestured for the landspeeder to clear, which its driver seemed to interpret as a greeting. "How's it goin'?" asked the ponytailed man, leaning out of the driver's side window.

Ezra stopped on the roof above, seeing more stormtroopers arrive on foot and on the other crate-loaded speeder bikes. It was now clear that this ponytailed man also wanted those crates. But confronting a stormtrooper squad was madness. The hammer of the Empire would nail this man's coffin shut.

The prospect of death didn't seem to scare this man, though. He sprang out of the landspeeder and ran straight at the Imperials.

With one booted foot, the man kicked the lead rider off his bike, then spun, blaster drawn, and fired at the oncoming squad. Some troopers went down, but more came to take their fallen comrades' place and return fire.

The man had reinforcements of his own. The burly nonhuman lumbered out from an alley and demonstrated why Ezra was correct in not wanting to cross paths with him. The bruiser picked up a stormtrooper from behind and threw him into another trooper. Both soldiers crumpled to the ground from the teeth-rattling impact.

Ezra scanned for the third member of this team, the

one in the Mandalorian armor. She was nowhere to be seen. What was her role in all this, other than setting the speeder to blow? The man and the bruiser didn't have trouble dealing with the squad by themselves. They only had to finish off a few more stormtroopers before they'd be in possession of the speeder bikes and the hover crates.

The crates—they were the fulcrum of this whole altercation. If these strange people were willing to risk their lives against such ridiculous odds to gain them, Ezra could only wonder what treasures they contained.

He went to the roof's edge. The lead speeder bike hovered a few stories below, riderless, its two large crates tempting him. If he dropped onto its seat, the bike's repulsor should absorb the shock of his fall.

Thinking no more about it, lest he get cold feet, Ezra closed his eyes and stepped off the roof. His stomach seemed to go first.

He landed in the seat with a butt-numbing wham. The bike bounced on its repulsors, and he caught the steering rods to prevent himself from being thrown off. He opened his eyes to see the ponytailed man and the nonhuman bruiser sprinting toward him.

"Thanks for doing the heavy lifting," he said, and kicked the bike into gear.

Ezra swerved around the bruiser, ducking his wild swing, and sped into an intersecting street. He waved good-bye to the two as more stormtroopers charged.

Those troopers didn't delay either of them for long. Soon they both trailed Ezra on separate speeder bikes. And since he couldn't figure out how to operate his bike's blaster cannon, he had to rely on losing them in the maze of the city streets.

He drove through broken windows of an abandoned warehouse, then knifed through a narrow alley. Whenever there was a quick turn, he made it, tearing through clotheslines and skimming the tops of trash bins. But he couldn't ditch his pursuers; they were gaining. The contents of his bike's crates must be slowing him.

He slowed even more when something dropped and landed on his bike's crates. "Pretty gutsy move, kid, jumping without a jet pack," said the girl in the paint-splattered Mandalorian armor. Her helmet filtered her voice but didn't re-modulate it like with the stormtroopers.

Ezra revved the bike to shake her off. She did the job herself, firing a blaster at the couplings that held one of the hover crates. It detached from his bike.

"If the big guy catches you, he'll end you!" she yelled, falling away on the crate. "Good luck!"

Ezra glanced back to see her hop off the hover crate and push it into an alley. He considered turning around, until the ponytailed man and the bruiser zipped past her, right on his tail.

He jammed his heel against the pedal. With one less crate, the bike accelerated faster. His vision narrowed. Walls and buildings blurred by him. He veered around a statue, dove under an arch, and darted down another alley, letting his instincts guide him more than his eyes.

As good as his instincts were, they didn't help him avoid the troop transport that blocked the mouth of the alley. Stormtroopers were posted on the ground, ready to fire at him.

All he could do was bob, weave, and hope he wasn't hit. A single, well-placed blaster bolt was all it would take to end his short career.

That one bolt never came—not to him, at least.

A stream of heavy fire from behind blasted the transport, scattered the troopers, and cleared the way for Ezra. He zoomed out of the alley, looking at his two pursuers, astonished by what they had done. Only the Empire's best troopers could shoot with that kind of skill on speeder bikes.

Who were these guys?

CHAPTER 5

Who was this kid?

Kanan had asked himself that question many times on this crazy chase. Either the boy had military training of the highest caliber, or his talents stretched beyond the ordinary. There was no other explanation as to how he could avoid being caught by them and the Imperials.

The chase would end shortly, however. They'd reached the outskirts of Capital City, where there weren't as many alleys or obstacles the boy could use to elude them. Kanan and Zeb gave their bikes an extra kick and zeroed in on the kid's back.

High-pitched whines made both look behind them. Three stormtroopers on speeder bikes now pursued them.

Kanan shook his head. Imperials always had to make things more difficult.

The kid sped toward the freeway that funneled traffic in and out of the city. Kanan and Zeb shifted their bikes to follow, as did the troopers. Stop signs on the freeway entrance ramp slowed no one. Fortunately, there wasn't much traffic on that section of the freeway.

Kanan wrenched his bike to the side, dodging the troopers' shots while turning in the saddle to respond with his own blaster. He hit one trooper in the chest, causing both man and bike to fall off the freeway.

But another trooper's blasts found the boy's bike. Sparks sizzled and a repulsor flap blew off. The kid lost control. His bike careened over the divider into the opposite lane.

The troopers' fire made it impossible for Kanan to veer into the other lane without getting toasted. Kanan signaled to Zeb that they had to take out their pursuers.

Zeb peeled his bike around to come right at one trooper, surprising the man and knocking him off the bike. Kanan, meanwhile, pulled a detonation charge from his belt and cut his speed so the third trooper overtook him. "Okay, you caught me. I give up!" Kanan said.

The trooper cocked his head at Kanan, probably perplexed that Kanan would concede when he seemed to be winning the chase. To prove the point, Kanan lifted his hands from the steering rods in mock surrender.

"Just kidding." Kanan tossed the confused trooper the blinking detonator and gunned his engine, speeding away as the trooper's bike exploded.

Zeb caught up beside him. The Lasat scowled when Kanan signaled for him to watch the cargo. Zeb never liked quitting a chase, but Kanan had to be the one to go after the kid. He wanted to confirm if the kid's talents were real or if he was just lucky.

He pressed a button on the bike's controls and the crates detached from the couplers and fell away. Zeb halted his bike before the crates, muttering something about ending the kid for risking their operation. Kanan ignored him and swerved over the divider into the opposite lanes.

The kid had regained partial control of his bike and was on the move. Yet Kanan had a much lighter load, having dumped both of his crates. He rocketed past the kid, then looped around to fly straight at his young quarry.

The kid panicked and slammed on his air brakes, skidding horizontally. Kanan did the same, so the two faced each other, sideways.

"Who are you?" the kid asked.

"The guy who was stealing that crate," Kanan said.

"Look, I stole this stuff—whatever it is—fair and square."

"And you made it pretty far, kid. But I've got plans for that crate, so time to give it up. Today's not your day."

The kid tilted his head, looking at something behind Kanan. "Day's not over yet," he said with a smile.

Kanan glanced over his shoulder to see TIE fighters cutting through the clouds to bear down on them. Wonderful. Just what he needed.

The kid stepped on his foot pedal, rotated his bike, and whisked off. Kanan spun his bike around to give chase, into a hail of TIE laser fire.

He adjusted his altitude and direction, anticipating the TIE pilots' firing patterns to steer through the barrage unscathed. Uncannily, the kid matched Kanan's exact movements, tacking right and left to dodge the lasers. No, it was more than uncanny—it was as if Kanan and the kid were on the same wavelength.

This kid had more than just luck.

Kanan, however, could've used some luck himself when a TIE's lasers scored a hit on his bike, shorting out the inertial compensators. He lost momentum instantly and could do nothing as his bike fell.

"Have a good one." The kid gave a mock salute and

sped away as Kanan's bike crashed into the ferrocrete. The TIE fighter swooped around to fly after the kid.

Kanan picked himself up from the wreckage. He unfastened his comlink. "This is Spectre-1. I need a lift."

He wasn't done with this kid. Not yet.

Turning off the freeway into the grasslands, Ezra was feeling like an old pro on his speeder bike. Despite losing a repulsor flap, everything else on the bike performed magnificently. The thrusters responded to the slightest nudge of the foot pedals. The engine hummed even at the highest speeds. The contoured handgrips made the steering rods move with ease. He had to give credit where credit was due. The Empire always kept their equipment in tip-top shape—including their TIE fighters.

A blast skimmed by his head, centimeters away. The TIEs' cannons were powerful enough to destroy enemy spacecraft. If they got a solid hit on his bike, there probably wouldn't be enough wreckage to identify his remains.

Whatever was in that crate had better be worth it.

He weaved through the prairie mounds, eluding the TIEs' lasers. He might find protection and a place to hide in the mountains, but he'd never outrace the TIEs before he got there. The only other option was to slow down so the TIEs overshot him. Maybe then he could turn back toward the city and lose them in the alleys.

He didn't even get to lift his feet off the pedals before a TIE's lasers slowed his bike for him.

His bike began to smoke and shudder. His speed declined dramatically. The engine must have been struck. Ezra jammed his heels against the rocker pads and pulled back on the steering rods, trying to keep as much altitude as possible. If the TIEs didn't get him, gravity would.

The TIEs dove closer, peppering the area around him with laser fire. None hit, yet his bike's engine gave a horrendous, wailing shake. It was gone. Ezra pressed the cargo detachment button, then hit the brakes. He flew off the bike and landed with a thud in the grass. He didn't break any bones, but the impact still hurt.

He pushed himself up. Flames engulfed the bike behind him. The crate, however, had detached and safely hovered a meter or two away. One of the TIEs wheeled back toward him. He could see its lasers heating up, priming to score a direct hit—on him.

He didn't bother to run. He wouldn't have gotten far. If this was the end, so be it.

Lasers twanged, but not from the TIE. The Imperial fighter erupted in the sky in a great ball of fire.

A star freighter with diamond-like angles sailed through the explosion and slowed to hang right above Ezra. The cargo hatch opened and a ramp half extended, revealing the man from the square, his ponytail whipping in the wind. "Want a ride?"

Ezra stood there, partially in shock. This man had been trying to stop him before. Now he had come back to save him? It didn't make sense.

The man reached out a hand. "Come on, kid—unless you have a better option?"

The group of TIE fighters screaming back convinced Ezra he didn't. But rather than head to the ship, he dashed to the hover crate. He wasn't going to leave without it.

Ezra began to push the crate toward the ship. The weight of its contents strained his muscles. The ponytailed man shook his head in disbelief. The freighter started to rise as the TIEs drew near. They'd be there in seconds.

Ezra cranked up the hover crate's repulsors, then took it in his arms and jumped.

He didn't know why he did; he just felt that he should. Normally, he couldn't leap more than a meter off the ground without a pair of jump boots. And a hover crate's repulsors were weak, with a ceiling of only a few meters. Yet his jump took him higher than that. Much higher.

It wasn't natural. But it felt natural.

His legs relaxed. His body soared. It was as if a little voice inside him had been released to sing. It connected him to the world around him, which was ablaze with life and energy. The green grass on which he had snoozed so many times had sprung him upward like a trampoline. Tiny insects buzzed around him, the flutter of their wings giving him lift. The outstretched hand of the ponytailed man seemed to pull him to the ship like a magnet.

It all happened so suddenly, so unexpectedly, Ezra could scarcely believe it.

In that hesitation, the surge of force that propelled him vanished.

Ezra fell.

CHAPTER 6

The crate slammed onto the *Ghost*'s ramp, without the kid. Kanan looked around. TIE lasers whitened the sky. He sighed. The kid's leap had been an incredible feat but it had not been enough.

Perhaps Kanan had been mistaken. Perhaps it had all been luck to begin with.

Then the crate on the ramp moved. Two hands clung to its sides. One grabbed the edge of the ramp. Kanan watched, amazed, as the boy pulled himself over it.

Who was this kid?

Laser fire crackled in the air, too close for comfort. The kid shoved his crate into the cargo bay. Kanan retracted the ramp and closed the hatch.

Zeb and Sabine were unloading the other crates in the bay. After a glance at the kid's crate, Zeb stomped over and wrenched off the lid. Inside was a cache of assorted blaster weapons, mostly E-11 stormtrooper rifles, DH-17 pistols, a couple of hold-outs, and a stingbeam.

The kid's eyes widened at the sight of the arsenal. "Do you realize what these are worth on the black market?"

"I do, actually," Kanan said.

"So don't get any ideas," Zeb said.

"Ideas? These are mine," the kid said.

Zeb showed his teeth. "If you hadn't gotten in our way—"

"Can't help it if I got to them first." The kid stood on his tiptoes to challenge Zeb's vicious stare with one of his own.

Kanan stepped between the two. The last thing they needed was a fight while Hera was trying to outfly TIEs. "It's not who's first, kid, it's who's last."

The additional sublight engines came online, jostling the *Ghost* and her passengers. Kanan grabbed a crate to steady himself. They must be nearing the upper atmosphere. Hera probably needed his help.

"Keep an eye on our friend here," he said to Sabine and Zeb. He climbed the ladder into the central corridor. To play it safe, he verified that the surveillance system was working. Sabine usually did her own thing, and Zeb wasn't necessarily the greatest of babysitters.

Kanan hurried into the cockpit. Atmospheric clouds fogged the viewports. Hera pulled on the flight stick, taking the *Ghost* on a steep climb. "You said this was a routine op. What happened down there?" she asked.

Chopper, plugged into the shield controls, responded first with a chiding snortle. Kanan knew the droid was right—he, Sabine, and Zeb had screwed up—but this was not the time to lay blame. "Chopper, please. It's been a difficult morning."

"He has a point, love. We've got four TIE fighters closing in."

Love. Hera tossed that word about like it meant nothing. Years earlier, Kanan would've believed in her affection and told her how exceptional a pilot she was. Now he deflected her sarcasm with that of his own. "How about a little less attitude and a little more altitude?"

"No problem." Hera slapped the flight stick hard to one side as the TIEs opened fire.

Before the artificial gravity could adjust, Kanan was thrown across the cockpit into the side wall. He grimaced. "If I didn't know better, I'd think you did that on purpose."

She banked hard to the other side, avoiding a deluge

of lasers. This time, Kanan gripped a component handle to keep from falling.

"If you knew better, we wouldn't be in this situation," Hera said. "Seriously, what happened down there?"

Kanan pointed at a surveillance monitor. The cargo bay cameras were trained on Sabine, Zeb, and the boy. "*He* did."

Hera glanced up from the controls, continuing to pilot. "A kid tripped you up? Must be some kid. Spill it."

"Aren't you a little busy at the moment?" Kanan asked. Sensors showed the TIEs were about to make a coordinated attack run.

Hera's gaze didn't leave him. "Spill."

The internal display of Sabine's helmet showed her the kid's basic biometrics. He was definitely human, of average height and build for a boy his age, probably only a few years younger than her sixteen years. He must be right-handed, since he wore an energy slingshot on his left forearm. Below two blue eyes and above a constantly devious grin, his nose stood large and prominent, as if it had a jump start on a future growth spurt. Like that of most Lothal natives, his skin bore a copper sheen, and his shaggy dark hair, parted down the middle, hadn't seen the barber in some time.

He was most definitely a street kid. An urchin.

While she was examining him behind her helmet, he was also scrutinizing her. "Are you a Mandalorian?" he asked. "A real one?"

If he hadn't been a kid, she probably would have answered his question with her blasters. Mandalorians were unwelcome in the galaxy those days, ever since the Empire had outlawed their mercenary practice and occupied her homeworld of Mandalore. The few who still roamed the stars were usually armored impostors, which Sabine Wren was not. But the kid didn't need to know that. He didn't need to know anything about her or her people. She remained silent.

The kid turned to Zeb. "How about you? You some kind of hairless Wookiee?"

Sabine smiled under her helmet. That would get Zeb going. The Lasat felt indebted to the Wookiees for helping his people fight the Imperials on his homeworld, but he despised ignorant comparisons. It would be amusing to watch how the kid dealt with someone three times his size and ten times his strength.

"Is that what the Imps taught you at school? That we nonhumans all look alike?" Zeb growled, and planted his foot on the crate and wiggled his four broad toes. "Well, let me teach you a lesson. I'm a Lasat, and we don't think highly of little thieving Loth-rats like you."

The kid scooted to the edge of the crate. "I was just doing the same thing you were. Stealing to survive."

"You have no idea what we were doing," Zeb said.

"And I don't want to. I don't," said the kid. "I just want off this burner."

Zeb snarled his lips into a cruel smile. "Nothing would thrill me more than tossing you out. While in flight." He reached for the kid just as the ship shook, pounded by laser fire.

Sabine's feet remained anchored to the floor. Balance was one of the first things you learned as a Mandalorian. Zeb, however, toppled over and landed on the kid.

"Get off," the kid gasped. "Can't . . . breathe."

"I'm not *that* heavy in this gravity," Zeb said, picking himself up.

"Not the weight," the kid said, his face puckering. "The smell."

Sabine nearly laughed. The smart-mouthed kid was a true urchin, fearless to a fault.

Zeb's purplish skin burned red. He grabbed the kid and hoisted him up. "You don't like the air quality in here, eh? Fine. I'll give you your own room." He dragged the kid past Sabine toward the storage lockers.

The kid kicked and screamed. "Hey, stop! Let go of me, you brute!" If Zeb's reach hadn't been so long, he probably would've been bit. Like all street kids, this urchin fought like one.

Zeb opened the locker and shoved the kid inside. Before Zeb slammed the door, the kid looked at Sabine, as if she could do something.

She stayed her ground, scanning her helmet's readout. The biometrics registered a flush of heat on the kid's face. He wasn't completely fearless. His boldness was just a mask, like her helmet.

She wondered what he was hiding.

CHAPTER 7

Hera powered on the final sublight engine to lift the *Ghost* through Lothal's upper atmosphere. The TIEs ascended with her, trying to penetrate the *Ghost*'s deflector shields. She would've told Kanan to man a turret, except that as he described what he'd seen the boy do, he spoke with a certain charge and emotion she hadn't heard from him in a long time.

"Kid sounds impressive," she said. Impressive enough to make her consider that he might not be any ordinary boy—he might have talents beyond the norm. This put his life in extreme danger. The Empire viewed anyone with such abilities as a possible traitor.

"You're not thinking what I think you're thinking," Kanan said.

"He held on to a crate of blasters with a pack of troopers on his tail," she said.

"Because I was there to save him. He's undisciplined, wild, reckless, dangerous, and . . ." Kanan's litany trailed off. "Gone?"

She followed his eyes to the surveillance monitor. It showed only Zeb and Sabine in the cargo bay, repacking the crates for delivery.

Kanan clicked the intercom. "Where's the kid?"

"Calm down, chief," Zeb said, his gravelly voice coming over the speaker. He walked over to the storage locker. "He's in here."

Hera checked the sensors. Even with the boost to their engines, the TIEs were gaining, as were their lasers. The *Ghost*'s deflector shields could only absorb so much.

She took the *Ghost* on a series of quick turns, evading enemy fire while keeping the engines hot. Once they broke into orbit, she could prepare the jump to hyperspace. That was the only way they'd lose their pursuers.

Kanan didn't seem concerned about the TIEs. He leaned closer to the surveillance screen as if that would give him a better view. "Zeb, where is he?"

Hera glanced at the monitor and saw Zeb pop his head out of the empty locker.

"W-well," the Lasat stuttered, giving the camera a sheepish grin, "he's still here in the ship."

Sabine pushed past Zeb and inspected the locker herself. "Oh, he's in the ship, all right," she commed. Her helmet sent an image to the surveillance screen that showed the ceiling grill inside the locker had been removed. The kid must have climbed into the ventilation duct.

"Very creative," Hera said, glancing at Kanan. "Sounds like someone I used to know."

The warning sensors blared. A TIE screamed overhead, its lasers rattling the entire ship. Chopper blatted out a damage report. The *Ghost*'s hull remained unscathed, but the deflector shields were low.

Hera threw her full attention into piloting. Their conversation about the boy could wait. This was time for battle.

She didn't need to tell Kanan. He ran out of the cockpit toward the dorsal turret.

Ezra shook like a tuning fork as he crawled along the ventilation duct. The TIE's blasts reverberated through the duct, causing the thin panels he was squeezed against to vibrate ceaselessly. He thought his teeth would rattle loose, until the duct panel below him collapsed under his weight and he dropped.

It wasn't a long fall—much shorter than his plunge

from the building and his flip over the speeder bike—but it hurt the most. His chest hit the ship's hard floor while his backpack slid over his shoulders and struck him in the head. He regretted taking so many of Yoffar's jogans.

Ezra adjusted his pack, took a breath, and lifted his aching head slowly. Just his luck. He'd been only a half meter away from a soft landing in a big cushioned seat.

He pulled himself up into the chair, only then recognizing where he was. He had dropped into one of the ship's gun turrets. Welcoming him through the canopy was a black canvas of bright dots.

They weren't just dots, Ezra realized. "I'm . . . I'm . . ." he said, choking on his disbelief, "in space."

And he was about to die.

A TIE fighter roared past, so close he could see the solar collectors on its wing. Ezra slid in the chair as the freighter rolled, skirting green bolts of enemy fire. The turret's crosshairs displayed wireframes of three more TIEs racing from behind.

The intercom hissed with a silken female voice. "Shields are holding—for now—but you need to buy me time to calculate the jump to lightspeed."

A familiar masculine voice responded over the intercom. "Buying time now." The ponytailed man must be in the other turret, because lasers rang out and lanced the cockpit of a nearing TIE. It burst apart in a twist of metal and fire.

Ezra blinked, the intensity of the explosion giving him flash blindness. When his vision cleared, he found himself being yanked out of the cushioned chair and flung back onto the hard metal floor. He looked up to see the woman in the Mandalorian armor remove her helmet.

She wasn't a woman. She was a girl, not much older than he was, with large eyes, a pinch of a nose, and rainbow streaks in her hair that matched her armor plates.

His head suddenly didn't ache anymore.

She hooked the helmet on the seat arm, then sat down and got to business. After a few spins in the chair to track the enemies, she thumbed the triggers and turned a TIE into a starfield of its own.

Ezra was astounded. This girl handled a gun turret like a pro. He tried to deepen his voice to make it sound older, though without any Imperial affectation. "My name's Ezra. What's yours?"

Her answer consisted of wheeling away from him and firing. Before Ezra could ask again, he was lifted into the air by his backpack.

"My name's Zeb, you Loth-rat," said the bruiser,

right in Ezra's face. Ezra grimaced and had to turn his head. The Lasat's breath smelled like the city gutter.

"Calculations complete," said the woman over the intercom. "But we need an opening."

"Found one." Sabine didn't wait for the crosshairs to turn green when she pressed the triggers. A third TIE was blown to bits, clearing an escape vector for the freighter.

"Entering hyperspace," the woman said.

Those million dots of space smeared into a million lines as the freighter made the jump. Ezra's stomach, however, didn't. Fortunately for everyone in the turret, it was empty.

PART II
TO SPACE AND BACK

CHAPTER 8

Ezra squirmed in Zeb's grip as he was hauled into the cockpit. "Let go! You can't keep me here! Take me back to Lothal!"

The pilot, a green-skinned Twi'lek with flight goggles strapped to her forehead, turned from the controls. "Calm down. That's exactly what we're doing." Hers was the female voice Ezra had heard in the turret.

Ezra held up his hands to stave off that ludicrous proposition. "Wait . . . right now? With Imperials chasing us?"

"We lost the TIEs when we jumped," the Twi'lek said. "And the *Ghost* can scramble its signature, so they won't recognize us when we return."

Ezra dropped his hands. He had thought only military vessels had that capability. "That's . . . pretty cool, actually."

He scanned the cockpit. This *Ghost* was more than just pretty cool. It possessed components far more sophisticated than what he'd seen in mass-manufactured TIEs or transport vessels in the spaceport. There was even an orange-domed astromech droid, which rotated its photoreceptors at him. Maybe if Ezra stayed a little longer, he could nick some of this tech.

He looked back at the Twi'lek pilot. "So just drop me and my blasters outside Capital City and—"

"They're not your blasters," said a sassy voice behind him.

Ezra turned to see the Mandalorian girl enter the cockpit with the ponytailed man.

"And we're not going back to Capital City," the man added. "The job's not done."

If the man said anything more, Ezra didn't catch it. He was staring at the girl.

She didn't give him even a glance.

Night had descended over Capital City, and with it came Agent Kallus. He strode through the city square, all in gray, wearing a fleximetal cuirass that protected his upper torso and gauntlet gloves over his hands. His combat helmet had blast-proof cheek plates, which framed and focused his incriminating stare. Stormtroopers went out of their way to avoid him, though an AT-DP walker tilted its head as if in salute. Kallus walked past it, without acknowledgment.

This concentration of military personnel and weaponry was unnecessary, since the ones who had engineered the crate heist were long gone from the square. The troopers should be out combing the city streets, searching for clues about the thieves, not running amok here. This was but another example of the incompetence he would have to reverse to accomplish his mission.

He came to the scene of the crime, where a group of Imperial officers huddled. He walked through the group without comment and inspected the smoldering wreckage. It confirmed what the forensics analysts had told him. Detonators placed on the speeder's carriage had caused it to explode. Moreover, surveillance footage from rooftop cameras revealed that a female in multicolored Mandalorian armor had probably planted the detonators, though it was difficult to verify from the angle. Kallus didn't need verification. A person of her description, with slightly different-colored armor, was already on Lothal's most-wanted list for causing similar havoc at an Imperial airfield.

What irritated Kallus was that she had done both deeds right under Imperial eyes. This wasn't the usual military incompetence—this was a gross neglect of duty that went up and down the chain of command. He had a lot of work to do to turn this planet around.

Aresko, one of the highest-ranking officers on Lothal as commandant of the Academy, came up beside Kallus. "They knew our protocol and were waiting in position."

"I've no doubt. You're not the first on Lothal hit by this crew," Kallus said.

Aresko exhaled a kept breath. "That's a relief," he said. "I mean . . . I assume that's why you're here, Agent Kallus."

Kallus removed his helmet. "The Imperial Security Bureau pays attention to patterns. When the Empire's operations are targeted on an ongoing basis, it could signify something more than the theft of a few crates. It could signify the spark of rebellion."

Aresko twitched, for good reason. Even the hint of rebellion on one's planet could instigate a change in leadership. Kallus knew the commandant would now do everything required to make sure that didn't happen.

Kallus toed the wreckage with his boot. "Next time they make a move, we'll be waiting for them—to snuff out that spark before it catches fire."

He stepped on the last bit of smoldering metal, crushing it to ash.

CHAPTER 9

Ezra emerged cautiously from the *Ghost* when the cargo hatch opened. Their landing site on top of a hill looked like everywhere else on Lothal: grassy and green.

Zeb pushed two hover crates down the ramp. "Outta the way, Loth-rat."

Ezra did as instructed, not wanting to be bowled over by Zeb's crates or the ones that came after. The pony-tailed man, whose name Ezra had learned was Kanan, pushed the crate of blasters they had stolen from him. Next to him walked the Twi'lek pilot. Hera. The astro-mech droid, Chopper, remained inside the ship, while the Mandalorian girl brought out a fourth crate.

She had not bothered to introduce herself.

Kanan and Hera headed down the hill. Ezra started to follow. He wasn't going to let them walk off with his blasters.

Zeb grabbed Ezra's shoulder and held him in place. "Hey," Ezra said. "Where are they going?"

"If I told you, I'd have to kill you. And I might just kill you anyway," Zeb growled. His fingers pushed deeper into Ezra's shoulder blade before he released him and moved on with his two crates.

"Grab a crate. Pull your weight," the Mandalorian girl said, her first words to Ezra since she had landed on the speeder bike. She nudged her crate past him.

Before she had taken twenty more steps, Ezra was pushing a hover crate out of the cargo hold. Chopper bleeped something at him but Ezra didn't take his eyes off the girl. He followed her and the others toward a settlement that lay below the hill.

The place looked barely habitable. It was nothing more than a collection of metal shacks, repurposed tents, and crude shelters made from shipping containers. Humans and nonhumans huddled in doorways or sat in puddles on a muddy street. Some moaned; others cried; a few wailed. All looked weary, hungry, and desperate. It was as if the poorest and most wretched people of Lothal had come to this one place to live—and die.

Kanan ordered the others to wait while he and Hera went ahead with the crate of blasters. Ezra didn't try to follow this time. He had a feeling if he did, those hungry faces might try to jump him. Better to stay behind with Zeb and the Mandalorian.

He took another look around the shantytown. He'd traveled throughout the grasslands, had ridden through some poor, isolated communities, but none compared to this misery. "Lived on Lothal my whole life. Never been here."

"The Imperials don't advertise it," the Mandalorian girl said.

Zeb joined in with a snarl. "Locals call it Tarkintown."

"It's named for Grand Moff Tarkin, governor of the Outer Rim," the Mandalorian girl said. "He kicked these folks off their farms when the Empire wanted their land."

"Anyone who tried to fight back got arrested," Zeb said.

Ezra remembered the arrest in the marketplace. Yoffar had spoken his mind, and in return, the commandant had charged him with that gravest of crimes. "For treason . . ." Ezra said.

A couple of the refugees shuffled toward them. Malnutrition had shriveled their bodies; exhaustion had wrinkled their faces. Ezra stepped back, clutching the handles of his crate. Zeb and the Mandalorian opened the lids of theirs.

"Who wants free grub?" Zeb asked. He reached into his crate and took out not a blaster, but a jogan fruit.

The shuffle became a scramble. Famished refugees rushed out from every hole and hovel for what was probably their first meal in days. Zeb and the Mandalorian distributed fruits and food packets to eager hands. Ezra stood stunned. Was this the whole point of stealing the crates? To help these poor people?

A pea-green Rodian in a brown jumpsuit put his puckered fingers on Ezra's shoulder. "Thank you," he squeaked through his snout. "Thank you so much."

Ezra stiffened. "I . . . I didn't do anything." He hadn't even opened his crate.

The Rodian didn't seem to notice. He grinned and walked away. More refugees assembled around Zeb and Sabine, some coming back for seconds and thirds, always grateful. Ezra stayed a few paces away from the crowd, somewhat uncomfortable. He felt bad for raising a fuss on the ship. He felt even worse for clamping up. He could count on his hand the people who had ever shown him any gratitude.

He left his crate to the refugees and wandered back to the *Ghost*.

Despite the research Hera had done during the flight, she had uncovered no explanation that satisfied her as to how or why the large stone slabs ringed the clearing she and Kanan entered. Such stone circles could be found all over Lothal on the various continents, without a hint to their purpose. During the Old Republic, these circles had been a matter of investigation. Archaeologists from all over the Outer Rim had come to examine them and decipher their origins. Speculations varied wildly. Some attested that the circles were proof that a ritualistic civilization had lived on Lothal millennia before scouts had logged the planet. Others surmised that the slabs were of much more recent placement, dragged together by the original colonists for use as a landing area in lieu of electronic beacons.

Under the Empire, all inquiries into the matter were terminated. Superstitious mysteries of the past had no place in the New Order. The stone circles were abruptly forgotten and left to weather the elements—which Hera assumed made them an ideal meeting point for Cikatro Vizago and his Broken Horn crime gang, or "syndicate," as he preferred to call it.

A number of dinged-up IG-RM war droids clunked out from behind the slabs. Though they appeared to be in shabby condition, Hera knew the state of their exterior casings did not impair their primary function—to shoot and kill. Vizago always had their weapons and interior circuitry well maintained.

Kanan stood tall, the crate hovering before him. He hid his distaste for being there behind an expression that was as cold and inscrutable as the stones. He loathed working with unsavory characters like Vizago, whom he considered self-motivated and untrustworthy. Hera had told him such alliances were a necessary evil, and that Vizago was fighting against the Empire just as they were. But she could tell he remained unconvinced. His eyes darted repeatedly to and from the droids as if he was gauging a speedy exit in case the deal went south.

Vizago walked down the path into the clearing, his arms wide in greeting, his sharp-toothed smile wider. The tips of the twin black horns twisting from the Devaronian's hairless head had also been sharpened, as had his long black fingernails. Multiple earrings pierced the upper cartilage of his pointed ears, lending him the guise of a devilish scoundrel. Hera received his embrace. Kanan did not.

Vizago took no offense. His beady eyes zeroed in on the crate. He pushed open the lid and his smile grew wider. "Any problems procuring these lovely ladies?"

Hera shot a glance at Kanan. They had agreed not to speak about the chase in Capital City. The less the Devaronian knew, the better.

"Nothing we couldn't handle, Vizago. Your intel was

accurate," Kanan said, then added under his breath, "this time."

Hera jumped on Kanan's last words so as not to arouse suspicion. "We got the goods and took a bite out of the Empire. That's all that matters."

Vizago closed the lid of the crate. "Business is all that matters. But I love that you don't know that." He gestured and a war droid came forward, carrying a container of credits.

Vizago took the credits and began counting them out to Kanan. He stopped halfway through their agreed amount for their payment.

"Keep going," Kanan said.

Hera tensed. The Devaronian had a reputation for being cheap, but she didn't think he was stupid. He'd get more than he bargained for if he tried to stiff them.

Vizago picked up another credit from the container. "I could. Or I could stop and trade the rest of the bounty for another bit of intel you've been begging after."

"The Wookiees?" Hera asked, unable to contain herself.

Vizago's red pupils centered on Hera. "The Wookiees," he said. His smile seemed anything but trustworthy.

CHAPTER 10

Ezra sat in the grass near the freighter and looked down the hill at Tarkintown. Questions filled his head. If the *Ghost*'s crew was truly on a mercy mission, why had it been necessary to anger the Empire by taking blasters? Couldn't they steal their food from someone else? Who were these people, really? Why was everything they did so hush-hush, so secret?

Why wouldn't the Mandalorian girl even tell him her name?

A breeze whistled through the grass. He drew his arms closer to his chest. They hadn't said how long they would be down there, and nights could be cold out on the prairie. He glanced back at the freighter. It wasn't any warmer in there. Hera kept the heating systems on minimal to evade infrared detection. These people didn't seem to mind flying around space in a cold ship.

The *Ghost*. It was a suitable name. The ship spooked him.

Ezra turned to look at the freighter. Something inside it tugged at him. It was the same uneasy feeling he had had in the town. It had brought him here, alone, and now was calling him inside. Could it be the answer to his questions? He had to go and see what it was.

He rose from the grass and ascended the ramp into the *Ghost*.

Shadows filled the cargo bay. Chopper must have dimmed the illumination. But Ezra didn't need eyes to know where he was going. He felt pulled, as if by a string. He went to the ladder and climbed into the main corridor.

Emergency lights glowed along his feet. Clunks and clangs echoed through the ship. The cockpit lay ahead at the end of the corridor, the instrumentation inside blinking on standby. Chopper probably had plugged himself into the monitors there. Did the droid hold the secrets? Ezra went toward the cockpit. But as he got closer, he felt farther away from where he should be going.

He stopped and turned around. An unmarked door was set into the corridor wall. He took a step toward it. And another. This felt right. Behind that door lay what had induced him to reenter the ship.

The door was locked. It would only stall him for a minute or so. As sophisticated as the cockpit's systems had been, this lock looked to be a much simpler device.

He reached into his backpack and pulled out his astromech arm. After tweaking the manipulator, he inserted it into the lock. He put his ear to the door and stilled his breath, listening only for the sound of the mechanism inside.

He jiggled the astromech arm back and forth. He heard nothing at first, then a faint click. The door slid open.

He put the arm back in his backpack and entered a room as spare as a monk's quarters. The bunk itself was a lean mattress without a blanket, as if no one slept there.

Someone did. Ezra could feel his presence drifting about the room. The ponytailed man. Kanan Jarrus. This was his cabin. And he had hidden something there.

Relying on his instincts, Ezra raised his hand and waved it through the air. His fingertips tingled and his palm felt like a rudder in a stream. The stream's current drew him under the bunk.

He bent down to touch the wall. It was smooth and cold but didn't give him shivers. Rather, he felt refreshed.

His fingers found a crack in the wall, too thin to be noticed by a casual glance. The crack made a right turn, then another, and a third, to form a rectangle. Was that what he was drawn to? A secret panel of sorts? He pushed his palm into the rectangle. Something in the wall clicked like the lock, and a drawer popped out.

A polygonal object sat in the drawer. Ezra picked it up, mesmerized. It reminded him of a chance cube from the betting gates at the spaceport, yet it was transparent and each of its many sides sparkled like a diamond. Maybe it was a puzzle. They were popular those days. He tried to twist its sides. Nothing moved.

He dropped it into his pocket. It might be worth something to someone, perhaps as jewelry.

He caught sight of a second object in the back of the drawer. He pulled it out.

The object was cylindrical, resembling a glowrod with a focusing lens yet missing the illumination bulb. It felt natural in Ezra's hands and he was compelled to swing it. As he did so, his thumb accidentally pressed a button in the middle.

To his astonishment, a sizzling bright blue beam projected from one end to nearly a meter in length. The object was by no means any heavier; on the contrary, it felt balanced. Waving the beam back and forth, Ezra had a clear sense of his surroundings, from the dimensions of the cabin down to the particles in the air. It was as if both his physical and mental reach had improved—as if the blade of light was an extension of his arm and his awareness.

"Careful. You'll cut your arm off."

Ezra spun around. Kanan stood in the doorway with Hera and Chopper behind him. The droid snickered in binary. Ezra frowned. He should've known better than to wander around with the droid in the ship. Chopper had ratted him out. And Kanan did not seem happy to find him in his quarters.

Ezra held the laser blade before him. "Look, I know you're not going to believe me. But it's like this thing wanted me to take it."

Kanan's eyes never moved, but they seemed to judge Ezra from head to toe. "You're right," he said. "I don't believe you. Now hand me the lightsaber."

"Lightsaber?" Ezra examined the blade in his hands. From some of the old spacers in the city, he'd heard tales of such weapons, laser swords wielded by mystical warriors during the Republic. "Isn't that the weapon of the Jedi?"

"Give it to me." Kanan held out his hand.

Ezra hesitated. Jedi Knights supposedly had special

powers, like being able to move objects and read minds. Maybe Kanan was one who had survived—if the Jedi had even existed at all and weren't just stories invented to put little children to sleep.

But Kanan didn't appear to be a Jedi. He didn't use any special powers to call the hilt to him. He waited with his palm open for Ezra to give the saber to him.

Ezra took one more swing, then thumbed the button to deactivate the blade. He felt small again. Almost claustrophobic. With great reluctance, he placed the blade in Kanan's hand.

"And get out," Kanan said.

Ezra lowered his head, not meeting Hera's eyes or Chopper's photoreceptors as he exited. Once he was in the corridor, however, his mood lightened. He took the mysterious polygon out of his pocket and squeezed it tight.

CHAPTER 11

Sabine poured herself a glass of bantha milk and leaned against the galley's countertop. The freighter's walls were thin, and she had heard the conversation in Kanan's cabin. This Ezra kid was quite a troublemaker, sneaking aboard and picking the cabin lock. She would've been more impressed if he had used a detonator on the door, but she was impressed nonetheless.

The kid entered the galley. He smiled when he saw her, but was too nervous to say anything, so she broke the ice. "Not too good at following directions, are you?"

That smile didn't leave him. "Not too much. You?"

"Never been my specialty." She took a sip of her milk.

Ezra stepped toward her. "Who are you people?" he asked. She gave him a raised eyebrow. "I mean, you're not thieves exactly."

"We're not exactly anything. We're a crew. A team."

She paused, struck by a question she hadn't fully considered before. "In some ways, a family."

Ezra stopped, which was good, because if he came any closer, she might have to tell him to back off. She didn't like her personal space invaded.

"What happened to your real family?" he asked.

That question she thought about every single day. It was like a charge that never stopped exploding. "The Empire," she said. "What happened to yours?"

The kid looked away. So that was what he was hiding. Something tragic had happened to his family. She sympathized; she knew the pain. But he'd have to let it go, and soon. The galaxy was a mean place and had no room for sensitive types.

Zeb lumbered through the doorway, trailed by Chopper. He looked past the kid. "Kanan wants us in the common room."

Sabine nodded and finished her milk. Zeb addressed the droid, pointing a stubby finger at Ezra. "If he tries anything, sound the alarm—or shoot him."

Chopper quipped back with a query. Sabine was also curious what the droid could shoot, since the only "weapon" Chopper possessed was an electro-solder that could function as a Taser.

"Shush," Zeb said to the droid. "Just watch him."

The Lasat clomped off. Sabine put down her glass and went to follow. At the doorway, she looked back at Ezra, who now seemed more like a doe-eyed boy than a master thief.

"Sabine," she said. "My name's Sabine."

His mouth opened to say something, but he was at a loss for words. She could tell he liked her. A lot. That could be useful if she needed anything done in the future.

Heading toward the cabin room, she heard Chopper snicker at Ezra. Funny how a droid knew more about the rules of human attraction than a human kid did.

"We have a new mission," Kanan said.

Zeb hunkered in the *Ghost*'s small common room next to Sabine. New missions were good things. He didn't enjoy being cooped up on the *Ghost*, keeping an eye on thieving human children. His place was out on the front lines, bashing together the heads of stormtroopers, doing to the Empire what it had done to his people.

Kanan continued his mission brief. "Vizago acquired the flight plan for an Imperial transport ship full of Wookiees they took prisoner."

Hera stood right next to Kanan. "We don't know if

they are the same Wookiees whom we were supposed to meet. Vizago couldn't confirm the prisoners' identities. But he had heard that most of the Wookiee prisoners were soldiers for the Old Republic."

This seemed to correlate with the name of the Wookiee soldier Wullffwarro that they had seen on the gunship. Yet for Zeb, it didn't matter who the Wookiee prisoners were. Wookiees were good people. Many had sacrificed their own lives to try to prevent the massacres on Lasan. "I owe those hairy beasts. They saved some of my people."

"Mine too," Hera said.

She had never opened up to Zeb about her past and he had never asked. But he suspected they shared a similar experience. The Empire encouraged slavery of her species, and he suspected that Wookiees had rescued Twi'leks close to her. Maybe they had even rescued her. He would not probe. If Hera wanted to reveal her background, she would in time.

"If we're going to save the Wookiees," Kanan went on, "we've got a tight window. They've been taken to an unknown slave labor camp. If we don't intercept this transport ship, we'll never find them. Now, I have a plan, but—"

Something clanked in the walls. Had a mynock

Ezra's tower is the perfect hideout—
and the one place he can call home.

Ezra spies on the
unsuspecting stormtroopers.

Kanan steals supplies from the Empire to feed the hungry people of Lothal.

Ezra discovers the weapon of a Jedi Knight on board the *Ghost*.

Hera gives Ezra some important advice:
"If all you do is fight for your own life,
then your life's worth nothing."

Zeb, Ezra, and Kanan run as fast as
they can from the Imperial soldiers!

THE REBELS OF LOTHAL:
Hera, Sabine, Zeb, Kanan,
Chopper, and Ezra!

Agent Kallus and
the forces of the
Galactic Empire.

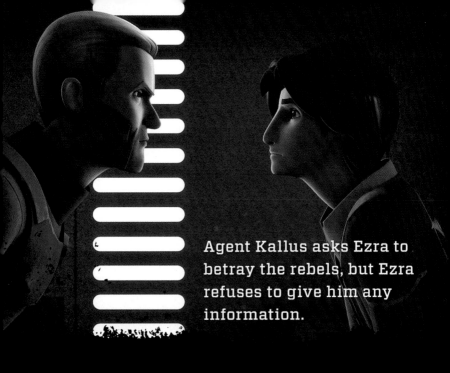

Agent Kallus asks Ezra to betray the rebels, but Ezra refuses to give him any information.

The *Ghost* zooms away from the Star Destroyer and makes the jump to hyperspace.

Wullffwarro tries to reach his son, but Zeb pulls the injured Wookiee away.

Ezra fires at Agent Kallus to protect Kitwarr.

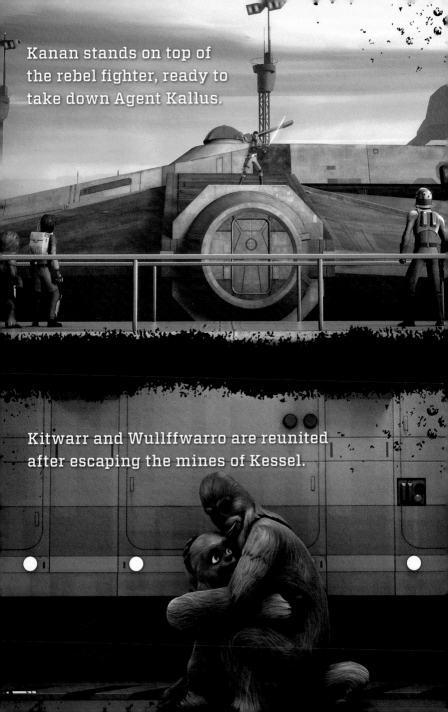

Kanan stands on top of the rebel fighter, ready to take down Agent Kallus.

Kitwarr and Wullffwarro are reunited after escaping the mines of Kessel.

chewed its way into the power cables? Zeb detested those parasites. They seemed to have no purpose in the galactic order other than to leech energy from starships and cause catastrophes.

Kanan pressed the button to open the supply closet. The Loth-rat Ezra tumbled out.

The others accused Zeb with stares. Kanan had assigned him to look after the boy, which wasn't fair at all. Zeb was an Honor Guard of Lasan, not a nanny. "I ordered Chopper to keep watch!"

Chopper trundled in, chirping excuses. He should've known better than to trust that droid. Chopper never obeyed instructions.

The boy scurried back toward the closet. Zeb grabbed him and held him in place. "Can we please get rid of him?" he growled to Kanan and Hera.

It was Sabine who spoke. "No. We can't."

Ezra stopped squirming and looked at her. Zeb recognized the kid's wide-eyed expression. *Karabast.* Teenage romance was the last thing they needed on the ship.

Sabine, mercifully, reciprocated none of it. She looked past Ezra to Kanan and Hera. "The kid knows too much."

The kid's body sank into Zeb's grip. Humans could

be such weak creatures when it came to rejection. On Lasan, if a member of the opposite sex didn't like you, you showed them your talents until they did.

"We don't have time to take him home anyway," Hera said. "We need to move now. I'll keep an eye on him."

Kanan shot her an unsure glance. At least he agreed with Zeb that this Loth-rat shouldn't be infesting the ship. But when Kanan nodded in approval, Zeb let go of the kid. If Hera wanted to babysit, that was fine by him. He had Wookiees to save.

CHAPTER 12

Ezra was getting used to hyperspace. His stomach didn't complain this time as the starlines streamed past the cockpit windows. Only his mind gave him trouble. It was hard to imagine that those starlines were planets, suns, or even other starships.

Hera sat across from him in the pilot's seat, checking and rechecking the navicomputer's coordinates. One miscalculation in their route could send them hurtling through a celestial body. In a breath, their lives would be over—and they'd never know.

Ezra didn't need to worry too much, Hera had assured him. She'd said that the hyperspace lanes were predominantly safe, mapped and tested by millions of pilots over millennia. What wasn't safe was what Hera and the *Ghost*'s crew intended to do after emerging from hyperspace. There was no way to test their plan.

"You know, this whole mission thing is nuts," Ezra

said. "I'm not against sticking it to the Empire, but there's no way I'd stick my neck out this far. Who does that?"

Hera pulled the lever to emerge from hyperspace. "We do."

The starlines vanished. In their place loomed a boxy starship with powerful engines. It wasn't big enough to store TIEs inside; instead, four of those fighters were racked onto the starship's underbelly. Ezra swallowed. His stomach started to panic.

Hera keyed the comm. "Imperial Transport six-five-one, this is *Starbird*, coming inbound."

Starbird was one of many fake identities the crew used for their freighter in situations like this. Only a privileged few—like lucky, lucky him—knew the ship's official designation, the *Ghost*. Ezra wished he'd never heard of it. He'd much rather be back in his tower, stripping power cores from holopads.

A pompous voice, sounding just like the one from the propaganda holopads, crackled over the radio. "State your business."

Hera didn't miss a beat. "Bounty. We captured an additional Wookiee prisoner and have transfer orders to place him with you."

"We have no such orders," said the voice over the comm.

Ezra tensed in his seat. Hera gave him a reassuring smile and continued to speak. "That's fine. We already got paid—by Governor Tarkin." She paused to let the governor's name sink in. "If you don't want the over-sized tree-swinger, I'll jettison him here and let you explain to your superiors why the Empire has one less slave."

There wasn't a response. The transport ship floated there, guns forward, pilots visible in the attached TIE cockpits. Hera had her hand on the hyperspace lever, in case they needed to jump again. It would be a random jump—not safe at all.

"Permission to dock," came the voice. "Bay one."

Ezra sat back, relieved. Perhaps these people did know what they were doing.

A few hours earlier, Kanan had made Zeb a babysitter. Now he wanted Zeb to be something even more preposterous. "Your plan's not going to work, Kanan. I don't even look like a Wookiee," Zeb said.

"You think the Imperials have bothered to learn the difference?" Sabine asked. She took Zeb's bo-rifle and leaned it against the bulkhead.

Kanan slapped binders over Zeb's wrist. "Just act like one."

Easy for humans to say. After this was over, Zeb was

going to lecture both of them on the many differences between Wookiees and Lasat.

He stood between the two at the *Ghost*'s airlock and held his head high, as he would expect a Wookiee to do. They never quavered in fear, even when taken prisoner. Zeb's hands were another matter.

"Stop flexing your fingers," Kanan said. "You'll bring attention to the binders."

"They chafe. You cuffed them too tightly."

"Poor Zeb," Sabine said from behind her helmet.

"Poor *you* if I lose circulation." If he couldn't move his hands, he wouldn't be able to bash any stormtrooper heads. They'd have to do all the dirty work themselves.

Kanan made a chopping gesture. Zeb quieted. The airlock door began to hiss open. He could see the white boots of two Imperial stormtroopers on the other side. He couldn't wait to see their white helmets.

When he did, both looked right at him. "That thing's not a Wookiee," said a trooper.

Zeb cursed silently. These weren't the usual, uneducated Lothal recruits.

"Haven't you seen a rare hairless Wookiee before?" Kanan said.

It stung Zeb that Kanan would use the kid's insult. Once they'd rescued the Wookiees, Zeb was definitely going to give Kanan a talking-to—with lots of angry growls and snarls for good measure.

For the moment, Zeb wailed, like he had heard many a Wookiee do. While he had the height and strength of a Wookiee, however, he did not have one's throat. His attempt sounded more like an Ugnaught's squeal than any sound a Wookiee would make.

The troopers exchanged looks and Zeb knew his career as an actor was over. "Oh, forget this." In one swing, he broke the binders and knocked both troopers through the airlock. They didn't get back up.

He grinned at Sabine and Kanan. "Told you they wouldn't buy it."

"You didn't exactly give them a chance to buy it," Sabine said.

"Couldn't help it. There's something about the feel of their helmets on my hands." Zeb rubbed his chafed wrists. "It's what a Wookiee would do anyways."

Kanan stepped through the airlock into the enemy transport. "Okay, you both know the plan. Move out."

Chopper wheeled out from the *Ghost* to join Sabine. The two went across the docking bay into one corridor of the transport. Zeb slung his bo-rifle over his back and hurried after Kanan down another.

★ ★ ★

Ezra leaned forward in his cockpit seat, listening to the comm. As crazy as this plan sounded, it was actually working. Kanan had even used one of his jokes.

"No troopers," Kanan reported. "Security's soft—"

A burst of static cut him off. Hera flipped switches. "Spectre-1, come in. Spectre-4? Spectre-5?" she commed, using their code names. "Comm's down."

Ezra watched as she made minute adjustments to the controls. She seemed to know every knob and dial in the cockpit, and there were hundreds of them. He'd been so wrong to think that if he could handle a speeder bike, he could pilot a starship.

"No, not down," Hera said. She gave up on her adjustments. "Jammed."

Ezra straightened in his seat, his instincts on edge. He stared out into space. "Something's coming."

Hera looked up from the communications console. There was nothing out the canopy viewport except the spread of stars.

"Ezra, I don't see—"

Emerging from hyperspace in the blink of an eye was the massive triangular vessel that had thundered over Ezra's tower. An Imperial Star Destroyer.

This was a trap. It had been all along. It was why Kanan and the others had boarded the transport so easily. The Empire didn't want the crew of the *Ghost* to get away this time. They wanted them in their grasp, in their ship.

Everybody was going to die.

Ezra sat, frozen in place. Hera knew that she had to act fast to save her crew. "Ezra! You need to board the transport and warn them!"

"What?" Ezra looked at her. "You want *me*? Why don't you do it?"

She was back at her console, turning all matter of dials and switches. "I need to be ready to take off, or none of us stands a chance."

"No," he said. "No way. Why would I risk my life for a bunch of strangers?"

She frowned at him, apparently insulted. "Because Kanan risked his for you."

She was right. Kanan had saved him from the laser cannons of a TIE fighter. But Kanan was also why he was stuck on this wretched ship in the first place. If he and Zeb hadn't chased after him on the speeder bikes— if they had just let Ezra have his crates—then his life wouldn't be in danger. Neither, probably, would theirs.

Ezra looked away from her. But her reflection regarded him in the cockpit's transparisteel. "If all you do is fight for your own life, then your life's worth nothing," she said.

Her words gave him pause. He pictured Kanan and

Zeb running down the transport's corridors, fleeing stormtroopers. He pictured the antique Chopper blowing a gasket, unable to move any faster. He pictured a hidden sniper scoping Sabine and pressing the trigger.

"They need you, Ezra," Hera said.

No one had ever needed Ezra. More to the point, he had never needed anyone else. He had prided himself on that. He was a lone operator, his own master. He listened to no one but himself and he did nothing he didn't want to do. If someone helped him out, that was their prerogative. If they didn't, he held no grudges. The universe hadn't done him any favors, and he preferred to do the same in return.

"They need you *right now*," Hera pleaded.

A shudder ran through the ship, rattling bolts and components. The Star Destroyer had locked its tractor beam on the transport and began to pull it and the docked *Ghost* into the gaping maw of the Destroyer's lower hangar.

Hera's reflection faded against the canopy's transparisteel. Now all Ezra saw was his own.

CHAPTER 13

Agent Kallus had Captain Zataire assemble a platoon of his best stormtroopers in the *Lawbringer*'s deployment bay. Kallus could trust these men. They weren't Lothal enlistees wearing the armor for the first time. To serve as a stormtrooper aboard an Imperial Star Destroyer, one had to be trained at an elite facility and pass a battery of extreme tests in a variety of environments. These stormtroopers had earned their place on the ship. They were the Empire's finest.

Kallus addressed them with three words: "Prepare to board." Their training had primed them for the rest.

He put on his helmet, took a blaster rifle from the weapons rack, and led the way toward the docking tube.

Hera marveled at the speed at which the Star Destroyer dispatched a wing of TIE fighters and hooked its docking tube to the Imperial transport. Such efficiency demonstrated just how the Empire had subjugated the entire galaxy in a short span of years. Toppling it would require more than the crew of the *Ghost*. They'd need a military force that could move even quicker than the Imperials.

This would be a long fight. And it might not be a fight they would be in much longer if Ezra didn't help them out.

She grabbed the boy's arm. "Listen. Our crew boarded that transport to selflessly rescue Imperial prisoners. They have no idea they walked into a trap. No idea what's coming." When he still didn't respond, she raised her voice. "You need to go warn them, Ezra—*now!*"

"It's too late for them. We should run while we still—"

"You don't mean that." She turned him around in his seat, made him look at her. To his credit, he did not flinch, did not look away.

"I do," Ezra said. "I swear I do."

She let go of his arm. This boy was more stubborn than Kanan. Yet he was also scared. He was, after all, just a kid. She shouldn't ask such things of him.

"Which is why I can't believe I'm doing this." Ezra stood up, tightened the straps of his backpack, and exited the cockpit.

Hera could believe it. Ezra might be stubborn like

Kanan, but he had the same heart, too. He was a rebel, deep down. One of them.

Kallus and his platoon stepped out of the *Lawbringer*'s boarding tube into the transport's docking bay. The captain of the transport, whose name Kallus had not bothered to learn, came forward. "Welcome aboard, Agent Kallus."

Kallus kept walking, as did his platoon, crossing the bay. The transport captain hastened to follow. "The rebels are headed for the brig, where quite the surprise awaits. I've positioned a squadron of stormtroopers there to capture them."

Kallus didn't even grant the man a look. The captain wanted a commendation he'd never get. Under the Empire, you did your job and kept your command. If you didn't, you faced the consequences of failure.

Kallus already knew the verdict that would strike this captain. It was why he had come aboard with his own men. It was why he hadn't learned the man's name.

He marched into the main corridor of the transport, leaving its captain in stunned silence.

Kanan took the lead as he and Zeb hurried down the transport's sleek gray corridors. So far they hadn't met any resistance except for a mouse droid Zeb squashed under his foot. Kanan veered around a corner and surveyed the transport's brig. A heavily reinforced blast door was set into the wall, but like the rest of the ship, the area was empty. "No guards on the door."

Zeb came forward and took up the position opposite Kanan at the blast door. "No worries. I'm sure there's one or two bucket-heads worth punching on the other side."

Kanan planted a detonator on the door. He hoped Zeb was wrong. For once it would be nice to slip in and out without engaging in combat.

"You sure the Wookiees are behind that door?" Zeb asked.

Kanan entered the activation sequence for the charge. "Where else would they be? There's only one brig on this transport."

"Guess you're right. They'd make holes through anything else." Zeb chuckled. "Nothing better than rescuing cooped-up Wookiees or what, eh?"

"It's a trap! It's a trap!" screamed a young voice. Kanan turned to see Ezra running down the corridor toward them.

"*Karabast*," Zeb snarled. "The kid's blowing another op!"

Ezra skidded to a stop. "It's not an op—it's a trap! Hera sent me here to warn you!"

The blast door started to open its multiple layers. White-armored bodies could be seen behind it.

"Run!" Ezra yelled.

Kanan and Zeb did just that. Ezra lifted his arm and aimed his slingshot. In its pocket force field formed an energy ball, which Ezra fired at the detonator.

The door exploded, blowing stormtroopers off their feet. Smoke billowed down the corridor. The three ran. Kanan tried his comm. There was no signal.

"We need to warn Sabine and Chopper, but they've jammed the comm," Ezra said.

"They'll follow the plan. It'll be fine," Kanan said. He wished he believed it. But that was what leaders did: kept the situation calm.

The boy was having none of it. "Yeah, 'cause the plan's gone just great so far."

As they turned the corner, a platoon of storm-troopers blocked their way, led by a man all in gray. Kanan recognized the uniform and rank insignia.

The man was an agent of the Imperial Security Bureau.

Zeb cursed under his breath. Kanan did the same. *Karabast*, indeed.

The transport's systems room was empty, like the corridors Sabine and Chopper had taken to get there.

Sabine wasn't complaining, but it seemed odd they hadn't encountered even one Imperial. Kanan had instructed her to use the comm only if there was an emergency. Since she hadn't heard from Hera or Kanan, everything must be okay on their end.

She went to one control station and motioned for Chopper to take the other. The droid complied, whining as he did so.

"Chopper, stop grumbling and work on that gravity generator." The droid always griped when communicating with Imperial machines. He found their logic cold and crude. Then again, Chopper whined about every machine he accessed, including the *Ghost*.

The computer security was lax and she hacked in with ease. The Imperial engineers clearly hadn't entertained the possibility that anyone would penetrate the transport's outer defenses and board the ship.

Her comlink made the faintest click. That was Kanan's signal. Not good. She started working faster with the gravity controls. "Bypass any stealth commands, Chopper. There's been an emergency."

Emergency or not, the droid grumbled all the same.

The agent and stormtroopers brought their weapons to bear. This only made Kanan run faster toward them, drawing his own blaster. "Don't stop," he shouted to Zeb and the boy.

They had only seconds before the enemies' guns were triggered. Seconds before they were dead. Unless—

Kanan didn't complete his stride. His front foot found not the floor, but a cushion of air. "Push off now!" he said, and leapt forward.

Sabine had heard his comlink click. She had turned off the artificial gravity right when needed. He flew down the corridor while the troopers floated off their feet, losing both their bearings and their aim.

Kanan fired his blaster, trying to clear a path. Only the agent managed to fire back, but he missed as Kanan barreled through the jumble of troopers, not loosening his finger from his trigger. Soaring behind him, Zeb hurled troopers right and left. Ezra held on to Zeb's foot, hitching a ride. Kanan was sure the Lasat appreciated that.

They sailed through the platoon, then down the corridor toward the docking bay. Kanan glanced back, seeing the ISB agent had turned around to fly after them. Ezra, meanwhile, had abandoned Zeb's foot to swim by himself.

"You okay, kid?" Kanan asked.

"You kidding?" Ezra said. He bounced off the floor and walls, tumbling over himself and gaining speed.

Even in dire situations, there was nothing like a kid in micro-gravity.

Sabine had been able to override the artificial gravity for a maximum of two minutes. It had taken her a quarter of that time to place the detonators on the control stations. But the trip back to the docking bay wouldn't take as long as it had on foot. Conveniently, she had Chopper, who was equipped for zero g.

She grabbed one of his legs. The droid ignited his booster rocket and they jetted out of the systems room. They met no resistance in the corridors and made it into the docking bay with seconds to spare.

"Five, four," she said, checking her helmet chrono, "get ready—two, one—now!"

Sabine braced herself as the artificial gravity kicked back in. She landed lightly on the docking bay floor before the airlock, while Chopper remained hovering on his booster. But the two stormtroopers whom Zeb had given a head-knocking went from floating in the air to dropping to the floor with a thud. Sabine suspected that would keep them unconscious until she and the others were parsecs away from there.

If the others had made it out of the brig, that was.

★ ★ ★

The sight of a purple Mandalorian helmet in the docking bay gave Ezra reason to cheer. They were all going to get out of this trap alive. And maybe, just maybe, Sabine would notice that he was the one who had saved them. Her congratulations would be a nice reward.

He sensed a fluctuation in the gravity and realized his low-gravity experience was about to end. He brought his feet underneath him and straightened.

"Now!" Kanan said.

Ezra landed with both feet on the corridor floor and didn't miss a step as he ran with Kanan and Zeb into the docking bay. Sabine was there, as was Chopper, on his rocket. Sabine craned her neck to look behind them. "Where are the Wookiees?"

"No Wookiees," Kanan said. "Sabine, you need to man the *Ghost*'s nose gun. Chop, go tell Hera to take off."

"Right," Sabine said. She hurried through the airlock into the *Ghost* without a word to Ezra. Chopper and Kanan went after her.

Disappointment slowed Ezra. Had Sabine even noticed he was there?

He must've been blocking Zeb, because the bruiser pushed him aside on his way to the airlock.

Ezra geared up to give the Lasat a shove in return. But he never made it into the airlock. Someone grabbed him from behind and yanked him backward.

"Let go!" Ezra cried. His abductor was none other than the Imperial officer in gray.

Zeb turned around in the airlock, drawing his bo-rifle. "Kid, get out of the way!"

"I'm trying!" Ezra said. He struggled, but the Imperial officer wrapped one arm around his chest, using Ezra as a shield. With the blaster in his other hand, the officer fired at Zeb, as did the host of storm-troopers rushing into the docking bay.

The blasts pushed Zeb back into the airlock. Ezra knew there was nothing he could do. Even this brawny bruiser he'd seen fling stormtroopers around like toy soldiers couldn't beat such odds.

"Sorry, kid." Zeb looked at Ezra with regret. "You did good."

The airlock slammed shut. The officer holding Ezra laughed. Ezra stopped resisting.

He shouldn't have stuck out his neck for those strangers. He had made the wrong choice, and now he was going to pay dearly for it.

CHAPTER 14

Hera had already warmed the engines when Chopper wheeled into the cockpit and beeped the go-ahead. She initiated the launch procedure immediately. "Airlock's shut. Detaching from the transport. We're out of here."

She held firm on the flight yoke, steadying the *Ghost* as it detached from the Imperial transport. "Chop, make yourself useful and jam their tractor beam."

Chopper retorted in annoyance but still plugged himself into the jammer. Being pulled back to the transport would eliminate their momentum and make them a ripe target for the Star Destroyer's turbolasers. They'd be space junk if they didn't make a quick getaway.

The transport broadcast a message from its captain. "Attention, rebel ship. Surrender or be destroyed. This is your first and last warning."

"Blow it out your exhaust vent. Literally," Hera replied. She channeled all available energies—including those that powered the turrets—into the engines. Shooting back wouldn't gain them much. Their lasers would be like pinpricks to a Star Destroyer.

What Sabine had planted would deliver a much bigger punch.

"Sabine, it's time," Hera said into the intercom. She poured on thrust, trying to get as much distance from the transport as possible before Sabine keyed her remote.

A moment later, the underside of the transport exploded.

Such damage normally would have been contained, except for Sabine's expert placement of the charges. The explosion in turn ignited a chain reaction across the transport. The portside hull blew open. The fuel line erupted. One engine brightened, then fizzled, while the boarding tube became a whoosh of flame that spread to the docked Star Destroyer. It provided Hera with the cover she needed to dive the *Ghost* under the Star Destroyer's nose and speed past.

"I can't see it from here," Sabine commed from the nose turret. "How'd it look?"

Hera had witnessed the explosion only on scopes.

Kanan had had the best view, since he occupied the dorsal turret. "Gorgeous, Sabine. As always," he said over the intercom.

Hera smiled. They had the best crew in the galaxy. With their young new member, they might even be stronger.

She pulled the lever to send them into hyperspace.

Weighed down by his backpack, Ezra huddled in the cold, empty cell of the Star Destroyer, brooding over his foolishness. How had he ever let Hera persuade him? He knew what it took to stay alive in this harsh galaxy. *Remain uninvolved. Rely on yourself and yourself only. Don't risk your life for others, because they won't do the same for you.* They were simple rules to live by. Ones that had not failed him in the past.

He had failed them. And in doing so, he had betrayed himself.

The cell door slid open. Two stormtroopers flanked the Imperial officer in gray. He had straw-colored hair and thick muttonchops that his helmet had previously covered. "I am Agent Kallus of the Imperial Security Bureau. And you are?"

Ezra smirked in defiance. "Jabba the Hutt." He might be in there because of his own stupidity, but he sure wasn't going to give the Empire any satisfaction.

Kallus's face remained impassive, as if he had never laughed at a joke in his life. Ezra had a sneaking suspicion that might indeed be true. Comedy was not the answer if there was any chance for him to get out of there. So he told the truth.

"Look," Ezra said. "I just met those guys today. I don't know anything."

The truth made no difference to Kallus. "You're not here for what you know, 'Jabba.' You're here to be used as bait upon our return to Lothal."

"Bait? You seriously think—" Ezra paused, laughed. "Wow, you're about as bright as a binary droid. They're not going to come for me. People don't do that."

Kallus said nothing else; he just looked down at Ezra. The man's stare was like a tractor beam: Ezra couldn't pull away.

Kallus brushed lint off Ezra's shoulder. "Search him. Then secure him here," he told the stormtroopers. He spun on a heel and walked out.

The troopers came forward. One yanked Ezra's backpack off his shoulders while the other grabbed Ezra's right arm and stripped off his slingshot. Ezra struggled in their grip. "Hey, get off me! Let me go, you goons!"

The contents of Ezra's backpack spilled out onto the floor. The first trooper scooped up the wrench, flashlight, and astromech droid arm and stashed them inside the pack. The second trooper pushed Ezra back onto the seating square. Then they strode out of the cell with his items, shutting the door behind them. Ezra was left alone once again.

He scowled. Not only did he feel foolish; he felt insulted. After all he had done, the Empire only considered him bait, just as the strangers saw him as a useful nuisance. "You need to go warn them, Ezra," he said, mimicking Hera's voice.

What had he been thinking?

He winced. Something jabbed his tailbone. He reached under him to find the polygonal object he had taken from Kanan's drawer. It must have fallen out of his backpack yet was too small for the troopers to notice.

"And, of course, the only thing I managed to hold on to is this worthless piece of . . ." His words stopped as his thoughts took another direction. The transparent object might be worthless, but it was also fascinating to behold. It weighed almost nothing, and each of its many sides was perfectly smooth, without cracks or creases.

Ezra sensed something was inside.

He pressed, pushed, and pried at the sides. That got him nowhere. He would need a blaster or a drill to pierce through that outer shell, and even with those tools, he'd probably destroy whatever was in there.

He tossed the stupid thing across the room. It bounced off a wall and rolled into a corner. Maybe one of the stormtroopers would trip on it. Then it would be of some use.

Ezra closed his eyes and lowered his head. He wasn't even angry anymore; he was exhausted. He cleared his mind, just focused on his breath. That always helped him relax. Perhaps sleep could take him out of this nightmare. He could wake up and find himself lying in the patch of grass around his tower, where green daisies grew.

The green daisies of Lothal were dazzling flowers. The presence of other forms of life made them bloom. The follicles on their stems were so sensitive that they could detect the breath or heat of a nearby organism. They would blossom for anyone who spent time to observe them.

He imagined peering at a daisy in the grass, watching it open its petals, slowly, like a child flexing its fingers for the first time. The spread of petals revealed a radiant center that shone emerald-like in the morning sun. The sight of this tiny wonder always revitalized him, no matter how hard his day had been.

"This is Master Obi-Wan Kenobi . . ." said a stoic voice.

As marvelous as the daisies were, they didn't have the ability to speak. Ezra lifted his head and opened his eyes.

The polygonal object lay open on the ground, as if its sides had been petals of a flower. From its center projected a miniature ghost of a bearded man in robes. His was the stoic voice.

"I regret to report that both our Order and the Republic have fallen, with the dark shadow of the Empire rising to take their place."

Ezra stared at the hologram. Though the robed man seemed somber and weary, as if he had just suffered a great loss, his voice and stature carried grace and nobility.

"This message is a warning—and a reminder—for any surviving Jedi. Trust in the Force. . . ."

The Force. What was the man talking about? Was this Obi-Wan Kenobi a Jedi? If so, might Kanan really be one, too? Or perhaps Kanan had killed Obi-Wan and taken his lightsaber. That seemed more logical based on how Kanan had treated Ezra, leaving him to rot in a

Star Destroyer cell. And why had this object opened in the first place, when it wouldn't before? So many questions. They were overwhelming. Questions to which he'd never get the answers.

The Force. His mind settled on those two words. He didn't know why. It seemed to be another thing he didn't understand. Another secret.

Yet deep down, Ezra sensed that this secret was also the answer.

CHAPTER 15

A quick jump into hyperspace could cause even veteran pilots to sweat buckets in their flight suits. Hera had made so many of those jumps recently she didn't break a sweat. Pulling the lever on short notice was beginning to feel like second nature. She'd have to make sure she didn't get too comfortable. Yet for the moment, she leaned back in her chair and watched the starlines. The Empire might control everything from the Core to the Outer Rim, but hyperspace was out of its grasp.

Her moment of peace ended when Kanan and a helmet-less Sabine entered the cockpit and dropped into seats beside Hera. "The whole thing was a setup," Kanan said.

"You think Vizago was in on it?" Sabine asked.

Hera had to nip any misgivings Kanan had about Vizago in the bud. "Vizago would sell his mother to

Jawas for a couple credits, yes. But we're a source of income for him. Odds are he didn't know."

Zeb also came in and took a seat, giving Hera the perfect opportunity to change the subject. "The kid did all right," she said.

"He did okay," Kanan said. He glanced down the ship's main corridor, then at Zeb. "Where is he?"

Hera also peeked down the corridor. It was empty.

"I, uh, thought he was with you," Zeb said.

Sabine swiveled in her seat. "What'd you do to him?"

Zeb shifted about, avoiding eye contact. "I didn't do anything to him," he mumbled. "That ISB agent grabbed him."

"What?" Hera and Kanan said in unison. No one had mentioned anything about an agent of the Imperial Security Bureau.

"The kid got grabbed, okay? He didn't make it off the transport," Zeb said.

"Garazeb Orrelios!" Hera said. She couldn't believe he'd leave the kid there. What had he been thinking?

"Oh, come on, we were dumping him after the mission anyway. This saves us fuel," Zeb said. His grin soon melted into a guilty frown. "They'll go easy on him. He's just a kid."

Appalled, Hera exchanged looks with Kanan. "We have to go back."

Zeb's eyes bugged out. "No—no, no! No way! You cannot be serious!"

She was more than serious. She started putting new coordinates into the navicomputer. "It's our fault he was there."

"Come on, Hera, we just met this kid. We are not going back for him," Zeb said. He turned to Sabine, pleading for backup.

Sabine looked away but whispered her agreement. "They'll be waiting for us. We can't save him."

Chopper, who was plugged into the corner and had been quiet the entire time, beeped a positive. Zeb spun on the droid. "What? What did that little dumpster say?"

Hera would have to give the droid a lubricant bath sometime soon. "He voted with me," she said. "That's two against two. Kanan, you have the deciding vote."

Kanan looked past her, out into hyperspace.

Ezra picked up the polygonal object. Its sides had closed after projecting the hologram and it seemed no different than before. He juggled it from hand to hand and rolled it around in his palms. If sold to the right person or organization, it would probably fetch him a shipload of credits.

Regardless, he was done feeling sorry for himself. So what if he'd made a wrong choice? People goofed up every day. He wasn't going to wilt and surrender because of it. He was built of sterner, smarter stuff than that. Stuff the Empire couldn't lock up. This Agent Kallus from the Imperial Stiff-faced Bureau didn't know whom he was dealing with.

Ezra Bridger refused to be anyone's bait.

Mulling over his options to break out of this joint, he took the best one available. He went up to the small set of stairs near the door and began to heckle the stormtroopers.

This wasn't your normal ribbing at the local podrace. Ezra used every joke in the book, poking fun at how the stormtroopers sounded and looked like clones, saying scout troopers had niftier armor than they did, even questioning their undying loyalty to the Empire. And he didn't stop. He repeated the same jokes, over and over, not trying in the slightest to be funny, only to get under their armor and annoy them to no end.

"You bucket-heads are going to be sorry when my uncle the Emperor finds out you're keeping me here against my will. I guarantee he'll make a personal example of you," he said. Ezra made choking sounds and added a few coughs for effect. Maybe the storm-troopers would think he was dying. That wouldn't be good for their bait.

The door opened. Ezra crouched beside the stairs as

the two guards rushed down into the cell. He leapt up the steps and was already out when they turned around.

"Bye, guys." He shut the door, pressing the lock button.

His first destination was the storeroom, which he found just across from the holding cells. It held more—much more—than just his backpack and slingshot. Imperial helmets of all varieties packed the room. He'd hit the mother lode.

As much as he wanted to collect the helmets he didn't have, his priority was to find an escape pod before those troopers radioed for help. He stashed the polygon in his backpack, strapped the pack onto his shoulders, and remounted the slingshot to his arm. As he turned to leave, his eyes fell on a smaller helmet, almost his size, made for cadets.

An idea struck him. He grabbed the cadet's helmet and put it on. It didn't possess all the advanced tech of a stormtrooper's helmet, but it had a simple radio tuner that automatically activated. He listened in on the comm chatter from the bridge.

"The delay was insignificant," an officer said. "The transport ship Agent Kallus diverted will dock on Kessel within two hours. The Wookiees will be offloaded to work spice mine K-seventy-seven."

Interesting, Ezra mused. The Wookiees had been

on that transport ship. They must've been locked in another hold.

"This is Stormtrooper L-S-zero-zero-five," radioed another voice. "Reporting for Agent Kallus."

"Kallus here." The man sounded even colder on the comm.

"Sir, th-the prisoner's gone," stammered LS-005.

"What?" snarled Kallus, a sliver of anger cracking his ice.

Ezra bit his lip. He couldn't leave the way he'd come. The corridor outside would be crawling with troopers soon. Spotting a ceiling vent, he began to climb up a stack of helmets.

"I knew the boy would act as bait, but I never dreamed the rebels would be foolish enough to attack a Star Destroyer. How did they get aboard?" Kallus asked over the comm.

Ezra stretched on his toes to reach the ventilation duct. He was listening but not paying much attention as he pried loose the vent's grille.

"Sir, the rebels didn't free him," radioed LS-005. "He, uh—"

"Agent Kallus!" shouted the officer from before. "There's a security breach in the lower hangar!"

Ezra winced from the volume of the man's voice,

nearly falling off the stack of helmets. He grabbed the edge of the vent and pulled himself into the duct.

"I don't know how," the officer continued over the comm channel, "but the rebel ship approached without alerting our sensors."

Ezra banged his head on the top of the air duct in shock. What rebel ship? The *Ghost* was the only one he knew. He knelt there for a moment. Had the strangers come back for him?

"Order all stormtroopers to converge on the lower hangar," Kallus said. "I'll meet them there."

Kallus's sudden change of attitude meant this was a serious breach. Maybe he was wrong about these so-called rebels. Maybe he had made the right choice in rescuing them, and now they were trying to do the same for him.

Right or wrong, he had to do something. The rebels were his best way off the Star Destroyer.

Ezra cleared his throat. He tapped the helmet to turn on the filter mic, then used his Imperial voice. "This is trooper LS-one-two-three, reporting intruders in the upper hangar. Sir, I believe the lower hangar is a diversion."

"Maybe, maybe not," Kallus replied. He didn't question Ezra's identification but also didn't fall for the entire trap. "Squads five through eight, divert to upper hangar. The rest converge as ordered."

Ezra sped up his crawl. Four squads were better than eight, at least. Every little bit helped.

CHAPTER 16

With all its systems operating in stealth mode, the *Ghost* slipped into the *Lawbringer*'s lower hangar unnoticed. Kanan knew their concealment wouldn't last. The hangar's security cameras would spot the unidentified ship—if they hadn't already—and the alarms would go off. He just hoped they could accomplish the rescue before every stormtrooper on the Star Destroyer arrived.

Kanan ran out as soon as the *Ghost*'s ramp hit the hangar floor, Sabine and Zeb with him. "Find Ezra. I'll be ready," Hera said from the hatchway.

Kanan surveyed the hangar. It was empty save for a bevy of cargo crates from a recent resupply. "Hold this bay until we get back," he told Zeb.

Sabine, with a blaster in one hand and a canister in the other, turned her helmet to the Lasat. "And this time, try not to leave until everyone's back aboard."

Zeb huffed. "That was not my fault!"

"Well, that's debatable," said a filtered voice above them. An Imperial cadet leapt down in front of Zeb.

The Lasat didn't blink. He just punched, smacking his fist into the cadet's helmet. The cadet was knocked backward across the hangar.

Kanan held back from firing. This Imperial seemed too short, even for a cadet.

The cadet stood and removed his helmet. "First you ditch me, then you hit me?" Ezra asked.

"How was I supposed to know it was you? You were wearing a bucket!" Zeb said.

The lightning of blaster fire preceded the thunder of four squads of stormtroopers rushing all at once into the hangar. The ISB agent led the attack, aiming his weapon at Ezra.

Ezra tossed his helmet at the agent, then joined Kanan and the others in a full-out sprint toward the *Ghost*. "Spectre-1 to *Ghost*, we're leaving," Kanan said into his comlink.

In the hatch, Hera laid down suppressing fire while they ran up the ramp. Ezra tried to aim his slingshot, but Zeb shoved the boy into the ship. "Oh, no, this time you board first."

Hera hurried toward the cockpit, which Chopper managed in her place. Once Sabine had made it through the hatch, Kanan commed the order: "*Ghost*, raise the ramp—and get us out of here!"

All around Kallus stormtroopers fell, taken out by shots. He ducked behind a crate for cover. The rebels firing from the freighter's hatch had the advantage of an upper position as the ship started to rise.

"Aim for the shield generator and engines," Kallus directed his troops. "Do not let them escape!"

His eye caught a pattern on the floor. Painted in orange was what appeared to be the outline of a bird lifting its head and spreading its wings. It reminded him of the legendary starbird, which perished in flames only to rise from its own ashes.

Why would the rebels have wasted time painting this? He reached down and touched the image, smearing it. He sniffed the fresh paint on his finger.

This wasn't just paint. This was sabotage.

"Take cover!" he shouted, and dove as far away from the starbird as he could. The next moment, the starbird exploded.

Troopers and crates went flying backward from the blast, then forward toward the giant hole that had been ripped open in the hangar floor. A vortex sucked everything not clamped down out into the vacuum of space.

Feet dangling, grip slipping, Kallus clung to the

edge of that hole as stormtroopers tumbled past him by the dozens. With all he could muster from his lungs, he called out to those troopers who hung on to handholds on the wall. "Turn on the shield!"

Whether the troopers heard him or not, they deciphered what he wanted. One stretched out and flipped a switch on a console.

Just as Kallus's grip loosened, an energy bubble shimmered around the hole. It sealed the breach and prevented him from falling.

Kallus crawled back onto the deck, watching the freighter zoom out of the hangar. He had to give his enemies a modicum of respect. They were more than your run-of-the-mill rabble-rousers. They were the real thing—fearless, daring rebels, willing to do anything and everything to achieve their mutinous ends.

As he rose, a stormtrooper approached, carrying the cadet's helmet that the boy had thrown at him. "Sir, one of the rebels was using this helmet. The transmitter was on."

Kallus was not a man who smiled. Yet when he took the helmet and stared into its black visor, his heartbeat steadied, and he felt the briefest pang of joy.

He knew where these rebels were heading.

And once he caught them, he was going to relish demonstrating why no one rebelled against the Empire.

* * *

Three quick hyperspace jumps in less than one Rylothian day—Hera supposed that must be a personal record. Settling back in her chair, she hoped to let that record stand for a long, long time. The perspiration that tickled her lekku was well earned.

The boy walked into the cockpit, a little sweaty himself. "Welcome aboard," she said.

"Thanks," Ezra mumbled. He hesitated a moment. Embarrassment blushed his cheeks. He spoke louder. "I mean, thank you. I really didn't think you'd come back for me."

She sat up and returned to her console. "I'll get you home now. I'm sure your parents must be worried sick."

The blush on his cheeks darkened. "I don't have parents. And you've got somewhere else to be."

Kanan, Sabine, and Chopper came in behind the boy. The cockpit was swiftly overtaking the common room as their meeting area. Hera would have to say something about this. She couldn't reach over bodies to adjust the controls.

"I know where they're taking the Wookiees," Ezra said.

Hera spun in her chair. "Where?"

"Have you heard of the spice mines of Kessel?"

More perspiration welled on Hera's lekku. This time

it didn't tickle. Of all the Imperial labor camps in the galaxy, Kessel was the worst.

"Slaves sent there last a few months, maybe a year, tops," Sabine said.

"And for Wookiees born in the forest," Hera said, "the mines are a death sentence."

"Then I guess we better go save them," Ezra said matter-of-factly.

Sabine gawked at the boy. Chopper telescoped his prime photoreceptor. Even Kanan's impassive demeanor was disturbed.

"'We'?" Sabine's eyes were as wide as ryll nuts.

"Come this far, might as well finish the job," Ezra said.

The kid was right, Hera knew. This was no time to rest on their laurels. They would probably never have another chance to rescue the Wookiees. She started to reprogram the navicomputer. "Setting course for Kessel."

Out of the corner of her eye, she noticed Kanan and Ezra exchange looks. Perhaps more than just the Wookiees could be saved on Kessel. Perhaps Ezra could help break Kanan out of the shell he'd hidden himself inside for many years.

PART III
KESSEL

CHAPTER 17

Little Kitwarr wanted to go home. Wherever he and his clan mates had been taken was the opposite of Kashyyyk. The forest here was made of metal, with piping for branches and smokestacks for trees. Men in white armor called stormtroopers pushed him and the other Wookiees along a grated walkway, which loomed over a dark, forbidding pit. It belched forth horrid, stinky clouds that made him wheeze. A yellow haze sickened the sky where there shone no sun, and ashes floated where birds should have flown. What little patches of land he saw were parched and cracked. Nothing grew.

Kitwarr began to worry that he'd never climb another tree in his life.

He cried out to his father, Wullffwarro, who had a group of the stormtroopers around him. The great

Wookiee howled that Kitwarr shouldn't lose hope. He'd find a way out of this, he promised.

"Keep moving," one man barked in Basic to Kitwarr's father. The others raised their guns at Kitwarr. He knew his father could throw all of them into the pit, but with binders on his wrists, Wullffwarro was powerless to do anything. Wullffwarro let out a mournful wail, then plodded forward down the walkway.

Kitwarr whimpered. It was the first time he'd ever doubted his father.

Standing with Zeb near the cargo bay hatch, Ezra checked his slingshot for the umpteenth time. Like before, it was ready for action. He, on the other hand, wasn't.

Once again, Ezra had made the dumbest mistake imaginable. He should never have suggested this mission. Even if the *Ghost*'s security countermeasures had slipped past Kessel's orbital safeguards, their small band could not match the firepower of a highly fortified Imperial detention facility. This was a suicide mission, plain and simple.

"Try not to get dead," Zeb said.

Ezra glared at the Lasat. What was the point of rubbing it in? He was only making matters worse.

Zeb snarled his version of a smile. "Don't want to carry your body out."

It took Ezra a moment to realize the big lug was joking. Ezra faked a smile back. If this was what soldiers called gallows humor, he didn't much care for it.

Sabine, ready for battle in her helmet and armor, and Kanan entered the cargo bay. "There's no place to land. You're going to have to jump onto the platform," Kanan said.

Ezra wished that this, too, was a joke. It wasn't. Kanan popped the hatch and the ramp lowered into a blizzard of blaster bolts. On the platform meters below, a stormtrooper squad had spotted the *Ghost* and commenced firing at it.

Kanan leapt out first, triggering his blaster as he went, followed by Sabine, Zeb, and then, with a swallow, Ezra.

The *Ghost* let loose its cannon, dispersing the troopers and allowing the jumpers to land safely on the platform. Ezra got off a few shots of his slingshot, then joined the others behind some mining crates. From there he saw the Wookiees being held prisoner beyond a line of shipping containers.

Kanan gave him the nod to proceed. There was no going back now. They were relying on Ezra to do his job, as he was relying on them to provide him cover from being blasted. The mission's success hinged on trusting each other—something that ran counter to what had kept Ezra alive in the past. Trusting strangers had only gotten him into trouble. Yet Sabine, Kanan, Hera, Chopper—even Zeb—weren't exactly strangers anymore. And there was no way a lone operator could accomplish this mission. It required a team, one in which he played a vital part.

Ezra ran toward the Wookiees.

Gunfire opened up all around him. He ducked and rolled, weaving between crates for cover, dodging blaster bolts by millimeters. Strangely enough, he wasn't afraid. He seemed to know the safest path instinctively and focused his gaze not on his surroundings but on the Wookiees who needed rescue. A giant silverback, whom Ezra had learned during the mission briefing was Wullffwarro, tried to break his binders while one cub looked at Ezra with bright, hopeful eyes.

It was that hope that pushed Ezra further. He snaked through mining equipment, darted across an empty stretch, then clambered up onto a shipping container and leapfrogged down the line. Blaster fire whizzed past him as he dropped in front of Wullffwarro.

The silverback Wookiee towered over him and growled, not in the least bit friendly. "Hey, hey, I'm here to help," Ezra said.

He pulled out his astromech arm and inserted its manipulator into Wullffwarro's binders. The manipulator fine-tuned itself and transmitted the proper codes to unlock the binders. Wullffwarro roared his pleasure once freed.

Ezra continued through the rest of the group, freeing Wookiee after Wookiee. Their cries of gratitude swiftly shifted to cries of battle as they stampeded the stormtroopers from behind.

The Imperials proved no match for berserker Wookiees, whose punches shattered armor and sent troopers screaming over the platform. The ones who didn't meet a Wookiee's fist were hit by the rebels' blaster fire instead. Soon the stormtrooper squad was no more and Ezra was running with the Wookiees toward the *Ghost*, hovering over the edge of the platform. The rebels joined them. Kanan gave Ezra a nod of approval.

Against all odds, this mission was going to succeed. Ezra had been wrong in thinking otherwise. Teamwork could do wonders.

Then four TIE fighters soared out of the pit.

A collective gasp was drowned out in a flood of lasers. Ezra dove. The TIEs blasted the platform, causing it to shake. Containers exploded. One shot penetrated the *Ghost*'s shields. The freighter wobbled and spun, and its forward laser cannon smoked, knocked out of commission.

"The aft guns, Hera—get Chopper to use the *Phantom!*" Kanan shouted into his comlink.

The *Phantom*, Ezra had discovered on his self-guided tour of the *Ghost*, was the auxiliary craft attached to the *Ghost*'s tail section. It featured twin laser cannons that could be used as an extra pair of guns if circumstances arose. This was one of those circumstances.

Hera must have already sent Chopper into the *Phantom*, because its guns responded almost immediately. Struck in a wing, one TIE spiraled back down into the pit.

It was replaced by something far more menacing—a boxy Imperial transport, rising out of the abyss on its repulsors and unleashing a barrage of laser fire.

The *Ghost* zoomed off, pursued by the three TIEs. Without access to an escape vessel, everyone on the platform scattered, searching for cover from the transport's cannons. Ezra crouched behind a crate and peeked over the side.

The transport landed on the platform and its bay doors opened. Agent Kallus emerged with another squad of stormtroopers.

"Take them down!" Kallus ordered.

The troopers rushed out, blasters blazing, while the little Wookiee cub meandered about in the middle of the platform, binders still on his wrists. Ezra pounded the crate in frustration. The cub hadn't been in the line of Wookiees he'd freed.

Wullffwarro leapt out from behind his cover, raising his arms and yowling. He ran toward the cub, whom Ezra guessed from the mission briefing must be his son, Kitwarr. But he didn't even make it a few paces before a bolt struck him in the shoulder. The big Wookiee fell to the platform floor. He moaned, hurt but alive.

Zeb rushed out to the Wookiee's side—and without thinking about it, so did Ezra. Kanan and Sabine shot at the troopers as Ezra helped the Lasat lift the dazed Wookiee to his feet.

"He'll be okay. I've got him," Zeb said.

Wullffwarro let out a pained growl. He wanted to keep going. Stormtroopers dashed after the Wookiee cub.

But what could Ezra do? He couldn't charge a platoon of stormtroopers. That truly would be suicide. The cub would have to look out for himself.

Ezra ran back to the crates.

* * *

A fireball erupted in the sky, showering pieces of a TIE onto the platform. Normally, Kanan would consider that a positive development. But the *Ghost* still had two TIEs on its tail, peppering it at close range with lasers, making it impossible for Hera to execute a proper pickup.

"I can't maintain position," Hera said, sounding strained over the comlink.

"Go. Lead the TIEs away and give yourself maneuvering room," Kanan replied. He kept firing at the troopers, giving Zeb cover to drag the wounded Wookiee behind the stack of crates. His efforts did little to thin the enemy ranks. The more troopers he and Sabine picked off, the more came forward. The only thing dwindling was his ammunition pack.

He looked around for inspiration of any kind. Something drastic needed to be done, or everybody was going to die very, very soon.

"I'm not leaving you behind," Hera said on his comlink.

"No, you're not," Kanan said. Nearby, a large shipping container lay open, having not yet been loaded with spice. "We're running a twenty-two pickup."

Sabine turned her helmet toward him. "Seriously?"

"You have a better option?" Kanan asked.

"Yeah," Zeb said. Having leaned Wullffwarro against a crate, he trained his bo-rifle at the troopers. "Jump into the pit and get it over with?"

Kanan didn't dispute the suggestion. It would be what they'd have to do if what he had in mind didn't work.

The *Ghost* burned its engines, jetting into the sky. The TIEs circled and followed. "All right, I'll be back," Hera commed. "Make sure you're ready."

Kanan let out a breath. No one could be ready for what he was about to do. Especially not himself.

Ezra came up beside him. "Twenty-two pickup? Can you let me in on the secret?"

"Kid, I'm about to let everyone in on the secret." Kanan assessed the battlefield one last time, then holstered his dying blaster and sprung over the crates to land on the other side.

Avoiding enemy fire, he unclipped two cylinders from his belt. They fit together as perfectly as they had when he had first constructed his lightsaber under the tutelage of Master Billaba, more than a decade and a half earlier.

Today, upon activation, the lightsaber produced a blue blade that blazed brighter than it had at any other time in that decade and a half. The stormtroopers ceased fire, as did Sabine, Zeb, and even Agent Kallus. All beheld Kanan in stunned silence.

Standing in the middle of the battlefield, with a hundred blasters pointed at him, Kanan opened himself fully to the Force.

He expected it to flood through him like a dam being released, as it had been a long time since he had completely freed himself to its light. He felt nothing of the kind. Instead, his heart calmed and his mind eased. The relief that came was subtle, subdued, like a gentle breeze that cooled on a hot day. A touch, a whisper, a sense of peace. He began to relax.

A web appeared before him, invisible but perceptible, linking all the beings on the battlefield to him, his life, his actions, his . . . *destiny*. Future and past events came to him in glimpses and sensations, none he understood, other than that he played a part in them—if he wanted. He could just as easily walk away and refuse.

The Masters at the Temple had often lectured about accepting your destiny. To Kanan, destiny had seemed a fixed matter. Its very nature implied that your future was defined, that you were a puppet acting out choices that had already been made for you. Yet upon seeing the web, how it moved and twirled and spun based on an infinite array of actions, Kanan realized he'd been wrong. Destiny wasn't a fixed matter. Destiny was a choice, a confidence, a belief. Perhaps all the Masters had meant was that by accepting your destiny you accepted yourself.

His friends on the *Ghost* had accepted themselves, while Kanan had been the one who had not. He'd hidden behind the lie that if he revealed himself, he'd put them all in grave danger. But they were already in danger, going toe-to-toe with the Empire. His friends gave their all to the fight, unafraid of what they might have to sacrifice. They needed Kanan to do the same. He couldn't fear what the Empire might do to him or them. The best way for him to protect their lives was to employ all the talents and skills at his disposal.

It was to use the Force.

Though he hadn't always been one with the Force, the Force had always been with him. He couldn't run away from it. He couldn't deny it any longer. He couldn't deny himself from himself.

Nor would the Imperial agent let him. "All troopers," Kallus said. "Focus your fire on . . . the Jedi."

Kanan Jarrus raised his lightsaber in salute. A Jedi he had been. A Jedi he would be.

CHAPTER 18

"Whoa," gasped Ezra.

Alone in the middle of the battlefield, Kanan Jarrus ducked, dodged, and deflected the blaster storm directed at him. He seemed to know when and from where each bolt was coming, jumping in the air at the right moment, curving his body to the perfect angle, or slashing his sword just in time. More than a few troopers crumpled, recipients of shots that Kanan deflected off his blade. Without even engaging in hand-to-hand combat, this one man—this Jedi—was holding off an entire platoon of stormtroopers.

Ezra stood there gawking, and the Wookiees didn't fail to notice, either. They picked up fallen blasters and joined the fight, roaring rage.

Kanan would have none of it. "Zeb, Sabine, get the Wookiees out of there—time to go!"

Zeb pulled a couple of Wookiees back from the battle. "Everyone, into the container!" He went to help the limping Wullffwarro, whose long, shaggy arm pointed toward the catwalk that connected platforms. Kitwarr hadn't been caught, but a stormtrooper was getting close. Wullffwarro bellowed in despair.

Ezra might not have understood the Wookiee language, but he knew when a father was imploring someone to rescue his child. And Ezra was the only one near enough to do it.

While the others hurried toward the containers, Ezra looked at Kanan. Though growing fatigued, the ponytailed man kept up his acrobatic defense against the stormtroopers. He had not flinched facing such odds. He was willing to sacrifice himself to save these prisoners, to save his friends, to save Ezra.

"If all you do is fight for your own life," Hera had once said, "then your life's worth nothing."

Ezra began a mad dash toward the catwalk and Kitwarr.

"Kid, stop!"

Zeb's cry reached deaf ears. The boy zigzagged through the crates and containers around the battlefield. Fortunately, he escaped the notice of the stormtroopers, who concentrated their fire on Kanan. Yet one set of Imperial eyes did see him: Agent Kallus turned from the fight to pursue.

Struggling to bring the stubborn Wullffwarro to the container, Zeb could not leave him to help the kid. "*Karabast!* I swear if he's left behind again, it's not my fault."

He knew Hera, Kanan, and Sabine wouldn't see it that way.

Another explosion lit the sky. Zeb hoped it wasn't the *Ghost*, though he couldn't tell at that distance. He shoved Wullffwarro inside the container, then spun around to give the stormtroopers a bo-rifle melody of his own.

In another gravity-defying leap, Kanan soared over the stack of crates to land on the other side. "Zeb, Hera's incoming!" He continued to block blaster bolts as he backpedaled toward the container. Sabine fired away, doing the same.

The explosion must've been one of the TIEs—which meant this crazy pickup might actually work. Zeb yelled at the Wookiees who had balked at quitting the fight. "Get in, you fur balls—now!"

The reluctant Wookiees got in, as did he and Sabine. Kanan entered last, whirling his blade to deflect stormtrooper fire. Zeb scanned the crowd inside. Everyone was there—everyone except Ezra and the cub. They hadn't made it back yet.

"Kanan, I think you inspired the kid to do, well, something you would do." Zeb indicated the catwalk in the distance, where Ezra chased after the stormtrooper and the cub.

The calm determination with which Kanan had confronted hundreds of stormtroopers cracked like a mask. He stood in the container hatch, lightsaber in hand, startled.

If Zeb knew of something that could've been done, he would've suggested it. But the *Ghost* would be there in a matter of seconds, as would the advance of stormtroopers. "Kanan?" Zeb pressed his friend.

"Seal the container," Kanan said with a sigh.

Zeb nodded and grabbed the container's hatch doors.

Kitwarr ran from the stormtrooper. The bridge over the pit was long and he was getting tired. His body wasn't made for running. It was made for climbing. Yet with binders on his wrists, he couldn't get a grip on anything.

Then one of the TIE fighters spiraled down from the sky, crashing into the bridge in a fiery ball. Metal rumpled, supports ripped free, and the section of the bridge

Kitwarr was headed down began to collapse. Kitwarr skidded to a stop, right at the edge, nowhere else to go.

He turned, finding that the stormtrooper was catching up to him. The stormtrooper had a gun in his hand, pointed at Kitwarr. Other troopers had done the same to his father and his father's friends. They wanted to hurt all Wookiees. He didn't understand why. What had Wookiees ever done to them?

Behind the stormtrooper, Kitwarr also spotted a human boy racing toward them. He looked like the same boy who had freed his father. Maybe the boy had a key for his binders. Maybe he could free Kitwarr. Kitwarr wanted to be free. He wanted to climb. The bridge floor beneath him was rumbling. It was going to crack soon. He cried out to the boy, pleading for help.

The stormtrooper turned and raised his gun at the boy. Kitwarr felt bad. He shouldn't have cried. He had alerted the trooper. The boy was human, but he had helped Kitwarr's father. Now the boy was going to get hurt.

The boy jumped. He jumped high in the air, somersaulting over the Imperial stormtrooper. It was amazing. Not even Kitwarr's father could jump like that.

The boy landed in front of Kitwarr. He winked, then turned toward the trooper and lifted his arm. Out popped what Kitwarr recognized as a slingshot, since he'd made many himself with twigs and rubbery vine. The boy's was made out of metal, and instead of rocks, it fired three energy balls.

All three shots hit the stormtrooper, knocking him back. The man stumbled, tried to raise his blaster again, but lost his balance and plunged over the bridge railing.

Kitwarr closed his eyes. He didn't like the thought of anyone falling—not even an Imperial stormtrooper—without being able to grab a branch.

The boy scooped Kitwarr up. "Gotcha."

Kitwarr felt safe in the boy's arms. He wasn't going to fall. The boy had started to unlock his wrists, as he had done for his father. Kitwarr smiled and opened his eyes.

A man in gray walked down the bridge toward them. Unlike the stormtroopers, his face wasn't masked under his helmet. And he wasn't smiling.

CHAPTER 19

Sabine would have much to argue about with Zeb after this was over. First of all, there was the matter of the kid, whom yet again he had let out of his sight. Then there were the Wookiees. Though Zeb hated the comparison, she thought they differed little from the Lasat. Excluding the Wookiees' fur, the two species were similar—tall, ungainly, and maddeningly stubborn. The Wookiees refused to follow her instructions to move and growled at her as she tried to push them to distribute their weight across the container.

She didn't bother asking Kanan for help. He leaned against a wall, eyes closed, looking utterly drained. He had earned a moment of rest after a performance in combat that rivaled those of the greatest Mandalorian warriors.

The container's ceiling clanged, much louder than the stormtrooper blaster bolts that pinged the walls from outside. The *Ghost* had landed atop the container. Sabine stopped pushing. The Wookiees would learn in a second why she had gone to so much trouble to move them.

"Magnetic seal locked," Hera said over the comm.

Zeb looked in Sabine's direction. "I hate this part."

The *Ghost* lifted the container off the ground and then took off at high speed. Yelping and yowling, all the Wookiees lurched into each other, one falling into Zeb.

Sabine stayed on her feet. The sight of Wookiees tumbling over each other would generally have made her laugh. Not today, not after what had just happened. As much as she might hate to admit it, she'd grown fond of the kid. She'd miss him pestering Zeb to no end.

The upper hatch opened into the *Ghost*'s cargo bay. Kanan sprang through it. Sabine wished she could use her jet pack to do the same. But she had work to do.

"Into the ship," she yelled to the Wookiees. The *Ghost* turned on its side and sent the Wookiees tumbling toward the upper hatch, making her job easier.

Kallus paused on the catwalk and watched the rebel freighter make a steep climb. The sole pursuing TIE replicated the maneuver with ease and fell in right behind the freighter. Yet what should have been an easy kill for the TIE turned into something far more tragic. The freighter detached its cargo container, which hit the TIE like a missile. The freighter sped away from the explosion, escaping once again.

He hoped the Wookiees were still in the container, but if they weren't, the loss meant little to him. Kallus had something the rebels would return for. He had the boy.

Why the rebels would risk everything to rescue the boy, as they had before on the Star Destroyer, made perfect sense now that Kallus had witnessed what the boy could do. Ordinary boys didn't break out of Star Destroyer detention cells. Ordinary boys didn't ride speeder bikes like champion racers. Ordinary boys couldn't leap over stormtroopers without wearing a pair of jump boots. This boy possessed a gift beyond the ordinary. It was a gift Kallus didn't have, but he knew the signs.

This boy, like the Jedi rebel, could command the Force.

Such an ability made the boy's capture all the more important. Certain entities in the Empire would find the boy of considerable value. Kallus would receive a commendation for the boy's capture, though awards weren't his goal. As an officer of the law, he had sworn a duty to protect Imperial citizens from those who posed a threat, which included all users of the Force.

The boy had his back turned to Kallus, using an astromech droid arm to unlock the Wookiee cub's binders. The binders fell from the cub's wrists and the boy put his astromech arm into his backpack. Kallus set his blaster on stun.

The cub saw Kallus and yelped. The boy turned. Kallus raised his blaster. "It's over for you, Jedi. Master and apprentice, such a rare find these days. Perhaps you are the only two left."

A sudden wind tousled the boy's hair. "I don't know where you get your delusions, bucket-head. I work alone."

"Not this time," said a voice, coming from below.

Kallus spun. The Jedi rebel, his lightsaber humming, stood on top of the rebel freighter, which had swooped low to rise from underneath the catwalk.

Kallus fired. Multiple times.

The Jedi's lightsaber deflected all the shots back at Kallus. Kallus's armor kept blaster bolts from burning through his chest, but it didn't reduce the power of their impact.

He fell backward, over the catwalk railing.

★ ★ ★

Safe again in the *Ghost*'s cargo bay, Ezra was relieved to let Kitwarr run free. The little Wookiee didn't realize how sharp his claws were. He had latched on to Ezra's shoulder as if Ezra were a tree.

Ezra forgot the pain upon seeing the reunion between father and son. Kitwarr raced into Wullffwarro's arms for a loud, howling embrace. The other Wookiees who packed the cargo bay added joyous roars as a chorus.

Ezra stood back, away from it all. A vision of his parents came to him and he quickly squashed it. Those memories only brought pain.

A hand squeezed his shoulder. Ezra looked up to see Kanan beside him. The man said nothing, just watched the Wookiees. On his belt, close to Ezra, dangled the hilt of his lightsaber.

For the second time that day, Kallus hung by his fingertips over an abyss. But in this instance his fingertips had a firm grip on a support beam under the catwalk. And the abyss wasn't a vortex trying to suck him into the ether of space. It was just a deep, dark mining pit. He'd still perish if he fell, but that wasn't going to happen. He had rebels to catch.

The only thing preventing Kallus from pulling himself back onto the catwalk was the stormtrooper who'd also fallen over the railing. The trooper clung to a lower support beam and was shaking the whole structure as he tried to climb up.

"First Jedi you've ever seen, sir?" the stormtrooper asked.

Kallus sneered. It had taken a ship to thwart Kallus, while this stormtrooper had been surprised by a mere boy. Such incompetence didn't deserve another chance in the Imperial ranks. He gave the man a good kick.

The stormtrooper lost his grip and shrieked as he plummeted into the pit.

When the support beams stopped vibrating, Kallus climbed onto the catwalk bridge. He brushed dirt off his uniform, then strode onto the platform.

Rarely did he fume with so much anger as he did now. In any case, it only made the situation worse for the rebels. They did not realize the forces now arrayed against them. For Agent Kallus always caught his criminals, no matter where they hid, no matter who they were, no matter whom he had to call or what he had to do.

Kallus would not rest until he caught these traitorous rebels.

CHAPTER 20

Ezra joined the *Ghost*'s crew to say his good-byes to the Wookiees. With Sabine translating their grateful roars, the hairy bipeds crossed through the airlock into a friendly Wookiee gunship Wullffwarro had contacted. The Wookiee soldier commanded a couple of such vessels devoted to freeing his people from slavery, but Ezra didn't inquire further. He was done with all the infighting between Imperials, rebels, and Wookiees. He just wanted to go back to his tower on Lothal, where he could eat jogans until his stomach hurt.

Wullffwarro and Kitwarr lingered last. The silverback bellowed so quickly that Sabine had a tough time translating. "Um, he says if we ever need help, the Wookiees will be there."

Wullffwarro reached out to rub Ezra's head. The touch was gentle, though Ezra could feel the strength under it. This Wookiee could squash him if he wanted.

Ezra smiled at the cub. "Good luck, Kitwarr. And try to stay out of trouble."

The Wookiees roared back and stepped through the airlock. Zeb sealed it behind them. "Trouble, humph. Look who's talking."

Acknowledging the Lasat's comment wouldn't get Ezra anywhere. He turned toward the others. "So," he said, keeping his smile, "I guess you drop me off next?"

Hera, Kanan, and Sabine exchanged surprised looks. Even Zeb seemed caught off guard.

"Uh, yeah," Zeb said. Did Ezra just hear disappointment in the bruiser's voice? The Lasat cleared his throat and regained his normal growl. "Finally, right?"

Not disappointment. Just surprise. Zeb was probably elated inside. "Right," Ezra said.

As he walked past the crew, he thought he heard Kanan sigh. But like usual, the man said nothing.

Then the *Ghost* wobbled as the Wookiee gunship disengaged, giving everyone a solid shake. Ezra used the opportunity to bump into Kanan and grab his reward.

"Oh, sorry," Ezra said. He didn't wait for Kanan to respond. He hurried into the corridor, slipping Kanan's lightsaber under his sleeve.

★ ★ ★

The prairie grass around Hera rippled back and forth like waves. She agreed with other pilots' assessments of the world. Lothal did indeed look like a sea of green.

Next to her, under the parked *Ghost*, Kanan scuffed his foot back and forth, lost in thought. She had assured him he had made the right choice in revealing himself as a Jedi. What was the point of fighting the Empire if he couldn't be the person he was meant—he was destined—to be? They were rebels, and they couldn't be afraid of that fact.

Surprisingly, Kanan had accepted her reasoning without argument. He couldn't go back on being a Jedi now. What bothered him was the boy.

"I thought he might make a good candidate," Kanan said.

"For running around with us? He's fourteen, he needs to be—" Then she realized what he was implying. "You want to train him?"

"Was considering it, until he stole my lightsaber."

Hera blinked. What little she knew about the Jedi was that instruction was a major part of their lives. Jedi were supposed to pass on what they learned, from master to apprentice. Kanan had only been an apprentice, but if teaching opened him up to his past, perhaps he should try it.

"Should I retrieve it?" he asked.

"No." She was surprised she said this. "Let him give it back to you like he did before. Let him make the decision for himself."

Kanan went back to scuffing his foot in the prairie grass. "What if he doesn't return it?"

"Can you make another one?" Hera asked.

A voice echoed inside the *Ghost*'s cargo bay. Zeb, Sabine, and Chopper were all in there, attending to their duties, but the voice was Ezra's. "So, uh, see you around?"

Hera moved closer to the hatch to peek inside. Sabine lubricated Chopper's gears and gave the boy an apathetic nod, though Hera could tell that wasn't how the girl actually felt. Chopper was more honest. He didn't emit his usual snort; he hooted softly, almost sadly.

Zeb put down the crate he was moving and gave Ezra a punch in the arm. "Not if we can see you first."

Hera knew that Zeb was just horsing around. Ezra didn't interpret the punch as anything like that. He rubbed his arm and headed toward the hatch, clutching the straps of his backpack. "Don't worry, you won't," he said.

Hera was about to nudge Kanan, but he stood tall now, his indecision gone, the grass below him straight, as if never scuffed. When Ezra was about to step off the ramp, Kanan moved forward. "I think you have something that belongs to me," he said to Ezra.

Ezra froze. For a moment, Hera thought he was going to buck and run like a frightened nerf. He didn't. He reached into his backpack and pulled out a transparent object.

"Good luck saving the galaxy," he said. He tossed the Jedi holocron to Kanan, then turned and ran into the prairie toward a distant communications tower.

Kanan did not follow him. He let Ezra go, watching him with regret.

Hera studied the holocron in Kanan's hand. It wasn't a perfect polygon anymore. Some of its sides had shifted. "He opened it," she said. "He passed the test."

She looked at Kanan. He had his own decision to make.

The ground floor of the communications tower looked undisturbed. Helmets lay strewn around the floor, shaken off their racks from the Star Destroyer's rumble. Propaganda holopads cluttered the workbench along with power couplings and droid brains. A forgotten jogan had rolled between the Treadwell base and the shuttle stabilizer fin. All was as Ezra had left it.

But Ezra didn't step past the threshold. He pulled

out the newest addition to his collection. Kanan's lightsaber.

He had decided not to sell it. Not now, at least. It would look good as a trophy on the wall, in between the various Imperial helmets.

Given time and practice, he could teach himself how to wield the blade. Maybe he could even teach himself how to hone this ability he had, what the holocron had called the Force.

Ezra's fingers squeezed the lightsaber. His instincts were suddenly on edge. Someone stood behind him. He didn't need to turn to know who it was.

After a moment, he asked Kanan the question that was burning in his mind. "What's the Force?"

"The Force is everywhere. It is everything," Kanan said. "It surrounds us and penetrates us. It binds the galaxy together. And it's strong within you, Ezra. Otherwise, you'd never have been able to open the holocron."

Ezra turned to face the ponytailed man. "What do you want?"

Kanan remained outside the tower, near a patch of green daisies. "To offer you a choice. You can keep the lightsaber you stole and let it become just another dusty souvenir. Or you can give it back and come with us, come with me, and be trained in the ways of the Force. You can learn what it truly means to be a Jedi," he said.

Ezra stared at the daisy patch. His instincts usually gave him guidance in situations like this. But he felt nothing at the moment. This was a decision he had to make on his own.

"I thought the Empire wiped out all the Jedi," Ezra said.

For the first time, Kanan's stony face cracked a slight smile. "Not all of us."

Ezra looked down at the lightsaber in his hand. He felt the metal pommel, the curve of the focusing lens, the button that activated its blade. He had heard that every Jedi built a lightsaber. If he believed this strange man, if he chose this path, would he be able to make one of his own?

When he looked up again, Kanan was gone. But the green daisies were in full bloom.

EPILOGUE

Aboard a Star Destroyer departing the planet Kessel, one ghost spoke to another.

Agent Kallus, however, was not a ghost. He only appeared to be by a trick of the light. The blue glow of the holographic figure whom he addressed gave his skin a pale, spectral sheen.

"Excuse the intrusion, Inquisitor, but in the course of my duties, I have encountered a rebel cell," Kallus said to the figure shimmering before him. "The leader of that cell made use of a lightsaber."

Irrespective of his present holographic form, the Inquisitor had the features of an apparition. He was dressed all in black, and his eyes glinted an eerie yellow, while the flesh of his tattooed face and bare, bald head gleamed a corpse white. If he wasn't the ghost of a man in armor, he was the closest thing Kallus had ever seen.

"Ah, Agent Kallus. You did well to call." The Inquisitor's voice lost none of its sinister oil through the convoluted routing of the Imperial Holonet. "Now tell me everything you know about this Jedi—and his apprentice."

In measured tones, Kallus made his report. He ended by vowing that he would leave no planet, no star untouched until these traitors had faced the Imperial justice they deserved.

In a dark cabin aboard a freighter parked on Lothal, there was another meeting of ghosts.

Bruises and wounds testified that the figure who sat on the bunk was indeed flesh and blood, yet Kanan felt anything but. Battle had exhausted his body, sapped his energy, and thinned him of the fear that had long paralyzed him. He wore a new mantle now, that of Jedi Knight, but by doing so, he had stepped into a phantom realm. Those who previously had worn the mantle, such as his former master and his colleagues, were dead. Long dead.

Was he, Kanan Jarrus, then the last of the Jedi? And how long would he survive before the Empire also exterminated him, making him another ghost?

The Jedi holocron in his palm projected what was,

in the technical sense, a ghost. In the air glowed a small hologram of a bearded man who spoke from the dead. He did not know how this Jedi had died, just as he didn't know how most of the others had met their fates.

"This is Master Obi-Wan Kenobi," said the hologram. "I regret to report that both our Order and the Republic have fallen, with the dark shadow of the Empire rising to take their place. This message is a warning—and a reminder—for any surviving Jedi. Trust in the Force."

Trust in the Force. That's what Kanan had done. But trust didn't vanquish worry. His revelation could—would—cause harm to the ones for whom he cared. They were all implicated now in his crime, and the Empire would not hesitate to hurt them to hurt him.

He sensed their presences about the ship, knowing what they were doing without seeing it, as all were creatures of habit. Zeb moved cargo in the bay, where Chopper would be making repairs on the laser cannon circuitry. Sabine drank her blue concoction in the galley. Hera, dear Hera, lounged in the cockpit, resting.

"Do not return to the Temple. That time has passed and our future is uncertain," the hologram said.

Time had passed; that was for sure. Enough that the Jedi Temple had become yet another ghost in his memories, an element of a dream he must piece together in his new life. A return to the Temple would not help, even if he wanted to go. Nothing of it remained on the world now known as Imperial City. Not a museum, not a plaque, not a mark. The Empire had reduced all its brick and steel to dust.

"Above all else, be strong," Kenobi said. "We will each be challenged—our trust, our faith, our friendships. But we must persevere, and in time, a new hope will emerge."

Hope. That was the key to all of this. To believe that freedom in the galaxy could be renewed. That tyranny was not eternal. That the dark side of the Force could not snuff out every flicker of the light.

Kanan believed. He had to believe. There was no other choice. But he was afraid. He sensed the tyranny of this Emperor was unlike that of any other despot history had ever recorded. His Empire would devour the whole galaxy if it wasn't stopped. This made the struggle Kanan and his friends were involved in the great battle not only of their lifetime, but of many, many lifetimes.

Perhaps it was the greatest battle of all.

"May the Force be with you, always," said Kenobi. After those final words, his ghost disappeared, and once again, the cabin was dark.

Kanan took a breath.

The darkness did not last. The door opened and in spilled light. A boy stood in that light. He held out a lightsaber.

Kanan went over to Ezra and took the lightsaber. In return, he put his hand on Ezra's shoulder. The boy beamed back.

In former times, a child of Ezra's age would be deemed too old to be an apprentice. But those times had passed. The boy had much to learn, as did Kanan. They would learn together.

May the Force be with them all.